RUM RUNNER

Also by A. M. Dunnewin

The Benighted Saga

The Benighted

Speakeasy Novellas

Speakeasy

Rum Runner

RUM RUNNER

A NOVELLA

A. M. DUNNEWIN

Dark Hour PRESS

First published in the United States of America by A. M. Dunnewin, 2014
Published by Dark Hour Press, LLC, 2020

Published by Dark Hour Press, LLC, California.

www.darkhourpress.com

Print ISBN: 978-0-9983929-9-8

Cover design by Dean Samed

Second Edition

This is for those who thought
the story ended.

Surprise!

CHAPTER ONE

. . . .

Charlie Rant couldn't recognize if the man lying on the hospital bed was a stranger or his brother.

"Did they tell ya?" a familiar voice breathed out, muffled from underneath the bandages.

Charlie blinked then, still trying to take in what he was staring at. The swelling in the man's jaw was the first thing he noticed next to the swollen eye, proof of the beating he had undergone. The dirty brown hair, same color as Charlie's, could hardly be seen through the dressings, while the once bronze skin was now splattered with bruises, deep purple blending into greenish-black. Charlie was already informed by the doctor that underneath the man's stocky build were two cracked ribs, a fractured wrist, and a broken leg.

"Yeah," Charlie finally whispered back, his forest-green eyes round and helpless. He had come back from speaking to the two well-dressed New Yorkers waiting on the other side of the door. Out in that cold hallway, the two men revealed something about his brother that Charlie didn't know about.

"Look, kid, we're not sure who laid their hands on him," one of them admitted. He was a taller man dressed in a black pin-striped suit with a new black fedora cocked over one eye. "This is the risk these rum runners take. If it ain't the law, it's other criminals. We're already startin' our own investigation on the matter, so no need to worry 'bout it."

"Are there any suspects?" Charlie questioned, looking from one gangster to the other. He would have been smarter to nod and leave things be, but he couldn't keep quiet, especially when his family was involved.

"That ain't yer concern," the other man insisted, a pudgier gentleman with a deeper voice. "Yer concern is our other shipment."

Other shipment. Charlie had no idea there was even one.

"I know I ain't much to look at," his brother interrupted. His voice croaked into Charlie's thoughts, obligated to make some witty comment to hide the pain.

Charlie simply shook his head. "No offense, Lionel, but ya look like a shitty wrapped mummy."

Lionel grunted, never one to laugh. In fact, that was usually how he expressed his amusement, and Charlie smiled to himself before the anxiety started in again.

"What are you and Travis doin' in New York?" Charlie asked, bringing up their childhood friend. "Why are you two tryin' to mix with mobsters?"

"It's none of ya business. Ya wouldn't understand, anyway—"

"You're right, I don't understand," Charlie admitted, his eyes watering beyond his control as his pent-up anger began to color his tone. He gripped the rim of his bowler hat a little tighter, trying to remain calm despite his body's physical reaction. "But now it is my business, so you're gonna have to tell me."

Lionel closed his eye, much like he did when he tried to block out something he didn't like.

"Why did ya agree to rum running?" Charlie asked again, trying to keep his voice even, to ignore the heat rising on the back of his neck.

His brother opened his mouth to speak, but closed it when the pain made his face cringe. He could only let out a groan to release some of the tension.

"Why?" Charlie repeated, his whisper becoming an irritable hiss. "And two shipments, Lionel?"

Lionel squeaked, and then his voice came through as he peered up at Charlie. "I need the money. Travis is helpin'."

"Ya couldn't have found some work in New Orleans? Ya had to travel all the way up here?"

"More money can be made here. They pay better."

"I could have helped—"

"Ya can't."

"Yes, I can," Charlie replied forcefully, though dropping his voice as he realized it probably carried. He stubbornly looked down at his brother's swollen and cut hand before continuing on. "I have some money saved. I can help get ya out of whatever it is you're in—"

"Not this time," Lionel's voice broke in, watching his little brother. "We're losin' the business."

"What?" Charlie gasped, their father's boat building shop instantly coming to mind.

"Hard times," Lionel sputtered, squinting as he held the pain back. "He didn't want to tell ya."

"Pa wouldn't keep somethin' like that from me."

"Well, he did," Lionel grunted. "Even for a country boy, yer still soft. Ya always were. Pa and I will make ends meet."

"I can help," Charlie seethed.

Lionel kept his gaze on his brother, his annoyance subduing into his agony. "Ya left us for a reason, the same reason yer trying to hide yer accent; too ashamed of us, the backwater county folk. But unlike ya, I'll suffer the consequences of my actions. About damn time ya suffer yers."

Charlie's eyes glittered as he stared back. They had already had this fight before, countless times. Somehow, he couldn't make him understand that education didn't mean abandonment; it meant opportunity and financial help, things he would eventually bring back to their family. Unfortunately, it never stuck well with his brother. To Lionel, education was a luxury, and if a relative didn't work hard to support his family, then he had abandoned them.

"Go on," Lionel sighed, his voice draining of emotion. "Go on, Harvard boy. Go back to where ya came from."

Charlie's throat tightened, but he didn't say anything as he pushed his chair back. With a heavy heart, he looked at Lionel one last time before leaving the room.

He wandered through the hospital hallways and out into the sweltering streets of New York City. Late summer still clung to the upbeat metropolis, and with the sun hanging overhead, Charlie didn't have to guess it was just past noon. Too hot to wear his coat, he peeled it off but put his hat on. It crushed his slick hair, which he had spent a good portion of the morning combing back with precision. His clothes were neither expensive nor cheap—black trousers with a matching fitted black vest over a deep blue shirt. He had saved up for the wardrobe which was supposed to fit his new and upcoming lifestyle. However, all his personal accomplishments fell to the wayside the moment Lionel opened his mouth.

Harvard boy. He would have been proud to be called that if it had been said by anyone else.

Charlie rubbed his eyes dry, and with the same set jaw like his father, held his feelings back and trudged on. His mother always called him the sensitive one, but it wasn't until his father and brother started in that he began to resent himself. Part of the reason he left home was to pursue his dream of becoming a big-time lawyer in New York City; to show everyone what he was made of. The other reason was to move away from his ignorant family. It was the first time Charlie admitted to himself that he really had abandoned them all.

He continued on through the brightly-lit atmosphere, the noon heat causing sweat to crease his brow. He used to marvel at the sight of the grand skyscrapers when he walked, but now they didn't exist to him. They were a backdrop to his over productive mind, along with the inhabitants who passed by him. It wasn't until a group of kids ran into his path that it startled him from his daydreams. They laughed as they ran off, and when he turned to see where they came from, he found the front of a corner drugstore. With the heat weighing down on him, the coolness of the soda shop beckoned him in.

Opening the door, Charlie made his way to the white counter, taking the only available seat in the middle of the hungry lunch crowd. Making himself comfortable, he draped his jacket across his lap and took off his hat. He was smoothing back his hair when the soda jerk approached him, asking what he'd like.

"Chocolate malt, please," Charlie answered, only loud enough for the man to hear.

With a nod, the attendant got to work on his order. Charlie folded his hands on the counter as a few of the customers left, giving him more elbow room. He used to glance around at people, wondering who they were and what kind of lives they lived. But now he stared straight across at the arched mirrors behind the counter, looking past the tiered sundae glasses and straight at himself.

It was while he was staring at his reflection when the front door opened behind him. In the mirror, he caught sight of a woman who stepped inside. Her mint green dress stood fresh against the working urban frenzy behind her, the front bodice being completely lace while the sides were satin, pressing against her curves. The lace skirt fell just passed her knees while a large satin layer wrapped around her hips. It was when she turned around to hold the door open for an older couple that he saw the rest. The satin joined together in an elegant bunch behind her with the leftover fabric falling down the skirt. The cream of her shoes and small handbag matched the cloche hat, its brim folded up with a thick beaded green belt wrapping around its base, finishing the ensemble.

Charlie knew it was impolite to stare, but he seemed to be in good company. The tone of the drugstore lowered, eyes peeking over at the woman as she turned back around and headed toward the counter. Everything about her was both beautiful and odd. Instead of the common bobbed haircut, her auburn hair was draped over her shoulder in long spiraling curls. Her actions were fluid, yet marked with a slight limp that caused her to lean against a gold cane for support. Despite the imperfection, she was still graceful in her movements. She had a Bohemian charm to her, which she carried all the way to the counter, coming to a stop at a seat right next to Charlie.

"Is this seat available?" she asked, her voice sounding like velvet in a room full of cotton and wool.

"Yeah," Charlie squeaked, having to clear his voice and start again. "Yes, it's all yours."

"Thank you," she smiled, propping her cane against the counter as she took a seat.

He had to admit that he loved her eyes. While they were hazel, the color reminded him more of a mint julep; cool golden liquor with streaks of soft green which were enhanced by the color of her dress. It was while he was taking in her soft features that he noticed the scars: three permanently jagged indents barely missing her eye and creasing the right side of her face.

"I'm glad to finally meet you, Mr. Rant."

Charlie blinked a couple times, slowly realizing she was addressing him. "Ya know me?"

The woman smiled with a sincere gleam in her eyes. "Your family owns a boat building business in the New Orleans area."

Charlie didn't realize his chocolate malt had arrived, and while she ordered her drink, he could only sit there and gawk.

"How is your brother?" she asked, pulling a cigarette case out of her purse. "I heard they did a number on him. Left his friend alone to witness it."

"They did," was all he could say, stunned by what she knew. "I'm sorry, but how do ya know my brother?"

She grinned a little, pulling a cigarette and retreating the case back into her purse, replacing it with a small matchbox. He recognized the logo from a ritzy restaurant he knew he'd never afford to eat at. "I don't personally," she was saying, "but I overheard about what happened."

Charlie pulled the collar of his shirt away from his tightening throat, glancing around him to help regain his composure. "How did you —?" he tried asking before her next words slipped in, cutting him off.

"I understand this may come as a shock since we aren't acquainted," she was continuing, striking a match she used to burn the tip of her cigarette. "I need to discuss this situation about your brother with you."

Charlie stared at her, feeling unnerved as she flicked her wrist and extinguished the flame. The attendant returned with a soda bottle in one hand and a plain glass ash tray in the other. He set both down in front of her, and only after she smiled in thanks did he stumble away to his next customer.

"Your brother is rum running for the Caprice family," her voice cooed, eyeing Charlie above her cigarette smoke. "I understand there's one more shipment he needs to deliver."

"How do ya know about that?" he asked quietly.

"I've had my own dealings with the Caprices," she answered, letting the cigarette linger between her fingers before taking a sip from the glass bottle. "Believe me, they'll kill him if he doesn't produce that shipment."

"They never said that," Charlie tried to reason. "They only said the shipment needed to go out. They never said they'd kill him over it."

Her face contorted into a modest scowl as she took a drag. "That was them saying it," she replied after she let the smoke blow in a stream above her head.

Charlie stayed quiet, stunned into silence.

"Your brother is a pack mule whose gone lame," she continued, a hint of regret in her tone. "If he doesn't deliver, they'll put him down. He's worthless to them, and knows too much."

"What makes ya say that?" Charlie wondered out loud.

Something flickered in her eyes. "Like I said," she replied with resentment. "I've dealt with them before."

Charlie swallowed the bile he could feel creeping up his throat, unable to stomach the chocolate malt still sitting in front of him. "So why are ya tellin' me?" he asked, taking a deep breath and smelling her smoke mixed with her airy perfume.

She tapped her cigarette, the ashes scattering into the tray. "I'm just as intrigued about who hurt your brother as you are."

"Really?" Charlie raised an eyebrow.

"Yes," she replied as she brought the cigarette back to her lips. "I have a suspicion, and I'm curious to see if I'm right or not."

Charlie eyed her as she took another drag, allowing the smoke to blow out her nostrils in elegant streams.

"Have you ever heard of the Durante family?" she asked.

"Sounds familiar, but I can't place 'em."

"They were rivals of the Caprices. Fought heavily over territory." She flicked the cigarette again, her eyes shadowing with a dark emotion. "Two years ago, the boss' nephew got an idea to set up the Caprices. It was a fake retaliation that would grant them not only respect from other families but also financial gains in the form of money and guns. This set up involved the planned death of the nephew's wife, which inevitably brought the retaliation to a head and made the whole plan work out perfectly. But unfortunately for the Durantes, the Caprice family learned about the truth, and they found their own way of retaliating."

Charlie realized that he had read about this story before. "A speakeasy," he mumbled, and when she raised her eyebrow, he admitted, "I read about it in the paper. The Durante family was found dead in a speakeasy they ran under their picture palace here in town."

She took another sip from the soda bottle and then brought the cigarette back to her lips, inhaling deeply before releasing the smoke back into the air. He saw that glimmer again in those eyes—tragedy and betrayal and something entirely different. "That's where all this begins," she said, eyeing him through the smoke screen.

"They all died, though," Charlie reasoned. "The mob boss, the capos—"

"They didn't kill them all," she replied, her eyes confirming it as she took a long swig from the soda bottle. "Someone survived."

Charlie took in a deep breath, glancing around to see if anyone was listening in.

"Whoever did," she continued, "is trying to resurrect the Durante name, gathering members who will follow. They aren't as big as they used to be, but they're growing. Enough to where they've helped steal shipments from rum runners. The last couple shipments were directly linked with the Caprices, which is why I have my suspicions. No one's ever dared to cross a Caprice shipment in a long time."

"And how would you know? You some sorta cop or journalist?"

"Focus, Mr. Rant," she warned gently. "It doesn't matter who I am. All that matters is saving your brother. You're going to need help."

"But why do ya care so much?" Charlie questioned. "Ya don't even know my brother or me."

The woman smiled, but it lasted only a moment so that it looked more like a wince. "Let's just say the Durantes are a huge pain in my ass that I'd like to take care of. Besides," she added as she smashed the remaining cigarette into the ashtray, "I don't like it when innocent people get caught in the middle of mob affairs."

"Is there a special reason for that?" he asked curiously, watching her open her purse and pull out enough to pay both their tabs.

"Personal experience," she replied as she put the money on the counter. Her eyes dared him to object when he tried to decline her paying for him.

Defeated, Charlie stared at the chocolate malt that was beginning to melt, paying attention to her from the corner of his eye as she finished the rest of her drink.

"The shipment needs to be picked up and delivered tonight," she concluded as she grabbed her cane and rose from her seat, half-heartedly dumping the matchbox back in her purse. "Enjoy your malt, and then go help your brother's friend get the boat ready. I'll meet you at the docks at eight."

Charlie didn't want to admit that no one told him where Lionel and Travis kept their fishing boat. But he was forced to ask since he couldn't waste the time searching for it himself. "What dock would that be?"

The woman acted nonchalant as she told him, "Port Richmond, over on Staten Island."

Charlie took a deep breath, trying to wrap his mind around things. As he watched her turn away, he asked "Do ya gotta name?"

Over her shoulder and without missing a step, she replied, "Its Katherine."

CHAPTER TWO

. . . .

Although his intentions were to change out of his nice attire upon reaching his apartment, Charlie just couldn't bring himself to do so. He didn't expect to feel the weight of the world heave itself on his shoulders, leaving him sitting on the edge of his bed with his revolver in hand. He contemplated the scenario, trying to comprehend how one brief conversation could change everything. The two brothers were really just country boys who had grown up in their family-owned business of fixing and re-building fishing boats. Now, Lionel had a debt hanging over his head that Charlie was going to have to pay to keep him, and himself, alive.

"How the hell'd we get here?" Charlie breathed, staring at the gun he always kept with his belongings. He glanced out the window, realizing the hours had slipped by and dusk was fast approaching.

He pulled the curtains closed before stuffing the revolver underneath the waistband of his pants. Buttoning his jacket up halfway, he checked to make sure he placed his wallet and keys in the inside pocket. Satisfied, he straightened himself

up, slapped his cheek to remind himself to keep it together, and left the room.

Outside, the lights of the signs started to glitter in the hazy August evening. Charlie, often in love with the ambiance of the nightlife, walked on with a purpose that left him stripped of distractions. Even the sparkling and colorful flappers who meandered across his path were just obstacles, and he passed by their shimmering and perfumed existence without a second glance.

Hailing a taxi cab, Charlie gave instructions to the driver with a pragmatic attitude, pretending that traveling to the harbor town at night was an everyday occurrence. Whether the driver cared or not, he didn't show any opinions as he started towards Staten Island, and Charlie secretly pulled out his wallet to make sure he had enough money for the trip.

His mind wandered as he was whisked down the streets, the skyscrapers standing tall like the intimidating gangsters he met in the hospital. Those two pinstriped shadows stayed in his thoughts until the ferry ride finally left them on the shore. And while the ferry drifted through mysterious waters with the moon reflecting in the dark currents, Charlie's mind drifted to thoughts of Katherine. Much like the river they crossed, she knew too much yet was the only lifeline in helping him get to where he needed to be.

Once on Staten Island, the cab driver pulled up to Port Richmond, snaking through quiet streets until reaching the area where the cars ended and the boats began. Paying the taxi driver with almost everything he had, Charlie walked down to the docks, hearing the taxi turn around and speed away. He watched his step as he made his way past the docked boats, searching for the familiar fishing boat his brother would have brought with him from home. Eventually he caught sight of it, stuffed in between two other boats with a little lamp glowing in the cabin. He let out a sigh of relief, glad he wouldn't be alone out there.

Anxiously, Charlie walked down the dock to where the plank was lowered. In the moonlight, he could make out the painted nameplate of the *Sandy Patty* on the boat's side, causing an overwhelming sense of home rush over him. He jogged lightly up the plank, and when he reached the wooden deck, he was met with the familiar bobbing as the boat rocked with the little waves that still came in from the North Atlantic.

"Travis?" Charlie called out, excited to see an old friend.

The boat creaked as it moved with no other sound except for the neighboring ships rocking along with it. Charlie checked the surrounding area, wondering if Travis was below deck and somehow didn't hear him. He made his way to the cabin, noticing the pile of sand bags gathered in a heap at the bow as he grabbed the lantern. To the right of the wheel was the opened hatch, and he used the short ladder to step down into the lower deck. Moving the lantern up so he could see, the light spilled across the confined space. The room was empty, waiting for the next cases of alcohol to transport. Charlie caught sight of a hefty mechanical contraption at the other end, and advancing towards it, lifted the lamp up further to expose what he saw. Before him was the boat's engine, enlarged and heavily modified, the sole reason the sand bags were needed at the bow to even out the weight. It was the type of engine that was never meant to be inside a boat due to its aggressive power.

Charlie felt his breath grow heavy as he moved back up to the cabin. Making his way across the top deck, he called out Travis' name, scanning the dock and nearby boats. Everything was quiet, and there were no traces anyone had ever been there except for the burning lantern. Charlie walked slower this time, keeping his eyes out over the railing. It wasn't until he reached the stern that he saw a small pile of sandbags sitting in the corner.

Taking a closer look, Charlie realized that a rope was tied around a couple of the sand bags while the rest were placed on top to anchor it down. The rope extended out over the boat's railing, and when Charlie tried to tug on it, the tension was too great to bend. Leaning over, he saw it disappear into the dark waters. He hung the light out over the boat's edge and found to his horror the hair of a man's head swaying just underneath the surface.

Charlie stumbled backwards, his free hand reaching for the handle of his revolver. He could hear his heart beating in his ears as his breaths quickened in panic.

"Cut the rope."

Charlie spun around. Standing on the other side of the deck was a well-dressed man in a suit and tie. His hands were in his pant pockets, and the hat he wore shadowed half his face. Charlie instinctively pulled out the gun and aimed it at the stranger. Noticing the man held no threatening stance, he couldn't pull back the hammer yet.

"What the hell's goin' on?" Charlie called out.

The man, whose tall frame remained straight and relaxed, shook his head a little. "The Durantes didn't leave him behind after all." He took a couple of slow steps forward, coming into the lamp light's perimeter with a cigarette hanging out of his mouth. "Ya must be the new sucker whose been recruited. Consider yerself warned." He nodded to the rope and the grim discovery that was made.

"I'm a friend of his," Charlie corrected. "Who the hell are you?"

The man shrugged but said nothing as he pulled the cigarette from his lips and blew smoke into the air. Charlie stared at him. He took in the man's dark hair which he brushed back when he readjusted his hat. He noticed how clean and tailored the black suit was, and how sharp the blue eyes were. When he still didn't answer, Charlie repeated himself, but something else answered in return.

The man's eyes rounded in slight surprise as the cocking of a gun clicked into the air right behind him. "It seems history likes to repeat itself," the man mumbled as he stuck the cigarette back in between his lips. "Good to see ya again, Kate."

The man pivoted around, and with the little light provided, Charlie could make out Katherine's form. She had changed out of the dress and into a black blouse and dark gray high waist pants he'd only seen girls at the beach wear. The long black jacket she wore was unbuttoned, and she had forgone a hat, leaving her hair pinned up into a sophisticated bun. Even from the distance he could see her eyes glistening with anger, staring over her own pistol at the man in front of her. Her other hand clutched the cane to help keep her balance. The man, still acting nonchalant, again removed the cigarette from his lips. He blew smoke at the barrel of her pistol while his other hand remained in his pant pocket.

"Didn't realize ya could put that thing on mute so well," Anthony commented, motioning with his eyes at her cane.

Kate kept her voice low while ignoring the comment. "What are you doing here, Anthony?"

"I should be askin' *you* the same thing," he answered back.

"Did you do this?"

"No, sweetheart, I didn't," Anthony admitted. His eyes never left her, and when he brought the cigarette back to his lips and inhaled, the smoke couldn't derail his gaze. His stare did gradually soften, but Kate knew that it was because he recognized the three scars lining the side of her face, knowing they weren't shadows.

"Don't call me that," she warned, though her voice remained soft as she put the hammer back in place and lowered the pistol into her coat pocket.

Anthony nodded in compliance, but said nothing.

Only Charlie was left to interrupt the silence. "How the hell'd ya know all this, about who did this to him?" he questioned Anthony.

"I came here to warn the lug that the Durantes would be comin' for him. Unfortunately, they beat me to it. So I hid, watching to see if anyone else would show up, and you, kid, didn't disappoint."

"Why did you think anyone else would be showing up?" Kate chimed in, her hard gaze revealing she was suspicious.

Anthony returned her stare as he said, "Because the guy who got tossed around didn't work alone. There was another hard head who worked with him, though he's probably headed towards the Pearly Gates by now."

"It's my brother you're talking about, and he ain't dead yet," Charlie blurted out angrily.

Anthony smirked. "Good to know, since I'm the one who interfered with that scuffle." He shifted his attention to Kate, and remarked, "Guess I'm just a saint these days."

Kate made no attempt to respond. All she did was look away as she shifted her weight against the cane.

Charlie slightly lowered his own revolver, stunned into submission though still keeping it pointed at the man. "You're with the Durantes?"

"That's what I'm makin' 'em think," Anthony mumbled, taking a deeper drag on his cigarette, causing the end to flare up. His eyes darted to Kate, but only rested on her for a brief moment.

Charlie didn't realize Kate had approached until she put her hand on his revolver, lowering it all the way for him. "We need to pick our battles," she whispered before staring behind him at the sandbags and rope. Her words made the adrenaline pump out of his system, and the physical loss of an old friend set in as he followed Kate's stare.

Seeing how the two acted, Anthony exhaled the rest of the smoke as he tossed the butt of the cigarette over the boat and into the water. He made his way around them, pulling a pocket knife out of his pant pocket. "We'll need to cut the rope," he explained. "He can't be pulled up."

"Why not?" Charlie wondered out loud.

"They bounded his hands and strapped some weights to his legs, heavy enough to lose the slack in the rope that's around his neck." Anthony peered over the edge before taking a step back and rolling his shoulders, working up his own courage to do the task. "He hanged and drowned," he confirmed, looking back at Charlie. "It'll be too hard to pull him out, especially now that it's dark."

Charlie witnessed in silent horror as Anthony sawed the rope, and when it finally snapped, Anthony put the knife back in his pocket and peered over the railing. "We're all clear," he announced, to which Charlie looked away.

Kate gently touched Charlie's arm, her own way of offering condolences. "I'm sorry to say it, but we do need to get going."

"He was our friend," Charlie quietly answered, trying to hold back as much of his emotions as possible.

"If you don't finish this," Kate reasoned, "your friend's death will be in vain." She motioned to the cabin with a nod of her head. "Go get us ready."

Charlie pursed his lips as he did what he was told, trying to recall his knowledge of boats while fragments of Travis' fate lingered among each thought.

Kate eyed him for a second before leveling her hazel eyes on Anthony. "What exactly are you doing here?"

"What haunts ya has been hauntin' me, too," Anthony responded, putting both his hands back in his pockets. "I was hopin' to warn that guy down there before they got to him, but by the time I arrived they were already smackin' him around deck."

"So it is true, then," Kate commented, squeezing the handle of her cane. "He's taken over."

Anthony bit back his response, peering out past the other bobbing ships and into the night. "Coast Guard is gonna be extra itchy out there," he commented, changing the subject. "They caught Alderman down in Florida last week. 'King of the Rum Runners' himself. Those patrol boys might be a little cockier now that they've captured a big fish."

Kate shook her head, hating his evasiveness. "We'll manage," she replied as she turned away, tired of looking at him and what he reminded her of.

"Well, either way, I'm comin' along."

Kate came to a sudden stop. "No, you're not," she stated, peering back at him.

"Look, I'm not a big fan of the Durantes, but I'm not a fan whatsoever of the Caprices. I can already tell there's pressure on that kid because of 'em." Anthony's eyes were burning intently as he spoke. "This boat is down a crew member, and it doesn't take a genius to know you two can't handle it on yer own."

"You have no experience on a boat," Kate reminded him coldly.

"I might not, but at least I'm not handicap—"

Kate's face twisted in rage as she limped towards him. She slammed the end of her cane down with each step, causing Anthony's hands to go up, half in apology and half in self-defense.

"Would you like to repeat that?" she growled, stopping right in front of him.

Taking a deep breath, Anthony lowered his tone into sincerity. "I'm sorry; I didn't mean it like that. But ya need help, and although I don't know much about boats, neither do you. I'm better than nothin'."

Kate's jaw clenched, but she decided to take her own advice and pick her own battles with him. So with bitter dignity, she pivoted back around and walked to where the plank was, trying to keep her limp less noticeable. Anthony held his tongue as he put his hands on his hips, watching as she fought against the cane. Ultimately, he turned away so the pity wouldn't show in his eyes.

Charlie, who had stepped out of the cabin then, noticed where Kate was. He observed with some curiosity as she carefully walked back down the plank, retrieving a large canvas tote bag that was waiting for her on the dock.

"Do ya need help?" he called out to her.

"No, thank you," Kate replied with a little heaviness in her tone. She faltered a little when she lifted the bag up by its handle, the weight giving her trouble. Sucking in a deep breath of stubbornness, she got a secured grip but then stopped short at the foot of the plank. She caught sight of Charlie's solemn movements around the boat, trying to prepare it for the trip. It made the weight in her chest overpower the weight of the bag she carried.

I'm so sorry, she thought, starting up the plank with her own burden to carry.

Upon reaching the top deck, she shuffled towards the cabin and laid the bag in the corner, out of the way. She knew the boat was unleashed from the harbor when Charlie came into the cabin. He closed the latch door so they wouldn't fall below deck, and then got behind the wheel.

"Anchor up. Plank up. Here we go," he mumbled, more to himself as he turned on the engine. It roared to life, louder and more powerful than he expected. The floor vibrated, rattling with intensity as he gripped the wheel just to hang on.

Kate leaned against the wall of the cabin to brace herself, surprised a boat could make such a ruckus.

"Whatcha got under the hood!" Anthony yelled over the noise as he stumbled into the cabin, unnerved by the engine roar springing up underneath the floorboards. "I didn't know a boat could make this much noise!"

"It doesn't," Charlie yelled back as he shifted the gears into reverse and started to pull away from the dock. "This engine's been swapped out for an airplane engine."

Anthony's infectious laughter burst through the air, springing from adrenaline the boat was shivering into his skin. "I guess we'll be flyin' to rum row then!"

Charlie laughed a little as the craft skimmed backwards, passing by the other boats. Coming to a stop, he shifted gears and proceeded forward, turning past the dock and leaving the area where his friend had been laid to rest.

CHAPTER THREE

. . . .

Out in the open waters, with the moon's bright path stretching across the glossy waves, Charlie was curious on how fast the converted fishing boat could move. However, it had been a couple years since he steered a boat, so he set a steady pace to regain his bearings. Kate still remained next to the wall, so he thought a conversation might help calm both their nerves.

"So, where exactly are we goin'?" he questioned, curious to see how much she actually knew. The gangsters had already given him instructions during their meet in the hospital, but he couldn't shake the feeling that Kate was somehow involved with them.

Already aware of why he was asking, Kate gripped her cane when the movements of the boat challenged her balance. "Just keep heading North-East," she finally replied, raising her voice above the engine noise. "We'll be meeting a schooner docked twelve miles out. They call her the *Shenandoah*."

"Twelve miles out?" he called back over his shoulder. "Long ways, huh?"

Kate slid along the wall closer to him. "Three years ago they changed the maritime limit, so now if you're within those twelve miles, you're considered illegal." She couldn't help smirk a little. "Being in law school, I would have thought one of your classes would have discussed this when it hit the news."

Of course she knows about law school, he thought, shaking his head a little. "I knew sleepin' in class would catch up to me one day," Charlie laughed, playing off her teasing tone. "So it's true what they say about these rum rows."

Kate caught sight of Anthony making his way back towards the cabin, finished with looking back at the harbor to see if anyone was following. "What about?" she asked, trying to act unaffected by his company.

"That they're lines of ships brimmin' with illegal liquor," Charlie replied.

"Pretty much," Kate answered. "They're probably brimming more than usual, though. That change in distance made things harder for smaller boats. A lot can happen in those twelve miles, and some boats aren't always equipped for the journey."

"Sounds like it was an act of God to move that line, then," Charlie commented, eyeing her playfully.

"No," Kate smiled, staring forward as Anthony came to stand on the other side of Charlie. "It was an act of Congress."

Charlie chuckled but said nothing more. He felt the tension forming around him, which only worsened when Kate left the cabin to go stand out at the railing.

Anthony heaved an unexpected sigh, but his tone was light. "So, kid, what do ya do in yer spare time?"

"I'm a law student."

"Oh, great," is what accidentally spilled out. Realizing too late, Anthony tried to quickly cover it up by saying, "I mean, good for you."

Charlie glanced at him, deciding not to respond. It seemed everyone liked to gawk at his choice of profession.

"So did ya do anythin' fun over the summer?" Anthony tried again.

Charlie decided to play along, hoping this would ease whatever had made them so uneasy. "Last month, I saw Babe Ruth make his 30th home run. How 'bout you?"

"I had the pleasure of seeing the Ziegfeld Follies on Broadway. Damn," Anthony breathed, chuckling a little. "Those girls know how to entertain! That show was as ritzy as it gets."

Charlie smiled a little, Anthony's enthusiasm rubbing off on him. "I guess I'll need to check out their show sometime."

"If ya do, invite me along," Anthony remarked. "I can help ya meet some of the girls backstage. Real dolls up in that joint."

Charlie would have added something witty, but when he caught Anthony looking over his shoulder at Kate, he decided against it. Despite Anthony's laid-back attitude, there was a longing about him that couldn't be masked.

"So," Charlie commented, deciding to cut to the chase. "You two have history?"

Anthony smirked, rolling his eyes as he mumbled, "Ya have no idea."

Charlie smiled a little as Kate entered the cabin, limping over to stand on the other side of him. "Is it normally foggy in a certain area like that?"

Charlie focused back on steering, realizing that a small dense cloud was fast approaching them, only hovering over a small spot in a clear night. "No," Charlie replied. "It's gotta be man-made."

"We should leave it alone," Anthony suggested, keeping his eyes on the hazy spot that grabbed their attention.

"It's in our path," Charlie pointed out, pushing the engine throttle to move the boat forward more. "We'll check things out as we pass by."

The *Sandy Patty* scooted faster through the deep waters, the fogged area growing closer. A smell lingered into the air, causing both Anthony and Kate to cover their noses.

"What's with the stench?" Anthony almost gagged.

Charlie already knew. "Someone poured engine oil on their exhaust manifold."

Anthony coughed, unable to hide his disgust for the odor. "Perfect way to create a smoke screen," he mumbled.

"Usually why people do it," Charlie replied as a small fishing boat came into view, smoke pouring out of its lower deck. Charlie slowed the throttle, the engine still purring loudly while coasting towards the stalled boat. Coming closer, the features of the boat became more pronounced, its paint wearing off and its life expectancy grim.

Kate gripped the handle of her cane, hugging the wall while watching the strange boat. Anthony went outside of the cabin, scouting for any movements on board.

"What the," Charlie breathed, squinting to see the faded name of *Mona* on the side of the ship. "This is Dugger's boat."

"Who's Dugger?" Kate asked, wishing the engine was quieter. The rumbling gave her chills.

"Who's Mona?" Anthony asked, smiling mischievously when Kate shot him a glare.

"He's a family friend," Charlie answered, steering them back around after they passed the smoking vessel. "And she's a topic we never discuss."

"Ya gotta lot of family friends out here," Anthony responded a little nervously, backing into the cabin.

Charlie ignored him, shutting the engine off. The vibrations fell away, leaving a deafening silence behind. "I didn't know he was out this way."

"Hey, we can't stop here," Anthony warned, alarmed that Charlie brought them to a stop right next to the dilapidated fishing boat. "There's a reason this guy put up a smoke screen, which I for one don't need to know about."

"He's a friend," Charlie insisted, making his way to the long plank of wood that was laid down against the side of the railing.

"Friends are disposable in this line of work," Anthony reminded him as he followed.

Charlie spun around, almost causing Anthony to run into him. "Mine aren't," he replied coldly. "I'm gonna help him if he's in trouble. He'd do the same for me."

Anthony backed off. Taking the opportunity, Charlie peeled his jacket off and threw it into the cabin before dragging the plank away from the railing to hoist it over the side.

Anthony shook his head while the younger man worked. With the same stubbornness, he put his hands in his pockets and peered at the craft bobbing in the water next to them. "Looks like more flotsam than jetsam is goin' on here."

Charlie didn't say anything as he lifted the plank up himself, sliding it across to the other boat's railing and securing it in place. He was starting to cross as Kate's cane made its rhythm against the dock, the light of the lantern hanging from her hand as she stopped next to Anthony.

"This isn't the time to be razzing him," she warned.

Anthony snorted in protest as he begrudgingly pulled his own jacket off, revealing a nice white shirt and black suspenders. Exchanging his coat for the lamp, he took a moment to look at Kate's face, the way the shadows danced across her features. "In case ya were wonderin', it means a wrecked ship and its cargo floatin' on the water rather than just cargo deliberately pitched overboard." Anthony gave her his devilishly handsome grin before adding smartly, "And ya thought I didn't know shit about boats." He turned away to follow Charlie when Kate's remark caught him off guard.

"Reading pirate books doesn't count."

"Says you," Anthony genially scoffed as he glanced over his shoulder and met her smug grin. "Just keep yer head down in the cabin. We'll be right back," he advised, readjusting his hat before following Charlie's path across the railings.

The journey was a little unsteady, and Anthony couldn't reach the other boat fast enough. Planting his feet on the rocking deck, he wiped the beads of sweat threatening his brow and caught up with Charlie who hesitated in front of the cabin. Holding the lantern up, Anthony saw what made Charlie stop: the latch was wide open, and constant smoke was trailing up out of the lower deck. Both men covered their faces with their shirts as they proceeded. Anthony passed through the smoke first, the lantern lighting the way as Charlie followed closely behind.

Inside was a hazy mess, and the first thing Anthony did was ram his knee into a wooden crate. He hopped to the side, cursing and rubbing the freshly bruised area.

"Well, I've been initiated," he grumbled while Charlie looked inside the crate, his eyes watering from the smoke.

Rummaging around, Charlie pulled out a bottle with no label on it, and held it up to the light, looking for any engravings on it. "I guess he made his own trip," Charlie's voice muffled through his shirt.

Anthony held his hand out, and Charlie gave him the bottle. Without hesitation, he opened the top and took a swig of the contents.

"Now would not be the time to drink it," Charlie lectured, bothered that Anthony was helping himself to his friend's stash.

"Even if I wanted to, I couldn't," Anthony replied, holding the bottle up. "This rum's been watered down. Whatever captain he got it from tried to stretch a profit. I bet you the whole batch is bad."

When Anthony let go of the bottle, causing it to crash to the floor, Charlie didn't feel so bad. Breathing into his shirt, Charlie continued through the smoky atmosphere, watching out for other crates that might be in the way. Anthony glided to the other side, holding the light up so they both could maneuver through the lower deck. Eyes burning and watering from the smoke, they only made it a couple feet before Charlie caught sight of a body lying towards the back, stuffed in between some crates.

"Ya see that?" Charlie called out.

Anthony looked over, taking a couple more steps to get a better view. He stopped in his tracks, however, as the light found two other bodies, blockaded and surrounded by the bootlegged bounty.

Anthony swung the light away from Charlie, who again tried to pick his way through the dimness he was left with. He didn't notice Anthony's eyes grew large at the sight, only how

Anthony backed away from the area. "We have to go," Anthony commanded.

"What do you mean—?"

"We have to go," he barked, walking hastily back to the stairs and taking the light with him. Charlie moved as best as he could to follow the path back, never seeing who lay among the crates or how they had died.

"The hell'd ya see?" Charlie demanded, rounding the crates and following Anthony up the steps to the top deck.

Anthony took in deep, coughing gulps of air before replying. He had only seen wounds like that once before, when he had stepped outside of a speakeasy and witnessed a man's body land on the roof of a Chrysler Six. When Anthony reached the railing, he squeezed his eyes shut. He remembered another body hitting the ground to the right of the car, sounding like a sack of flour as the head smashed in from the impact. Before his mind recalled how the blood crawled across the pavement, he opened his eyes and took in a deep breath of the salt air. Anthony regained his composure by taking one more deep breath, and then rotated around to find Charlie coughing behind him, still waiting for an answer.

"There were three of them," Anthony announced, his adrenaline dying down as he spoke.

Charlie was wiping the smoky tears from his eyes when he noticed that Anthony was too spooked to wipe his own.

"There were two more at the base of the engine," Anthony breathed in, trying to steady his nerves. "They've been dead for a while, which means they didn't die here. They were put here, and it ain't hard to figure out why." Anthony rubbed his eyes, adding, "I thought they would have followed us. But this? This is some serious plannin'." He had turned away to check the *Sandy Patty* when suddenly everything sounded quiet. Kate was missing. He hoped she was just hiding out in the cabin like he told her to.

"How serious?" Charlie questioned, the smoke still moving around them while the dead lay underneath their feet.

"I think someone knows," Anthony confirmed, stepping onto the plank and scuffling across. "Might have learned about our course from yer last family friend."

Charlie swallowed hard as Anthony reached the other side, turning back to hold the plank. Charlie made his way across, his legs wobbly as he moved. Upon reaching the *Sandy Patty*, his only thought was to get behind the wheel and put the modified engine to good use.

Just as he stepped off the plank, a bright light suddenly shot out across the deck, blinding him instantly. He came to a skidding halt, covering his face as everything around him went white. Anthony cursed from where he stood, dropping the lantern on the ground.

Both had been unaware of the small vessel that coasted next to the *Sandy Patty*, its size matching the boat it had paralleled itself against, giving it the advantage of going unseen. The haze of the smoke also did its part in keeping the attack private, as planned.

"The both of ya better remain where ya are," a thick accent directed from somewhere in front of them. "We got no problem sprayin' ya across this deck."

Charlie blinked as he tried to lower his arm from his eyes. His revolver was still pressed against his abdomen, a reminder of what he should have kept in hand. Anthony moved closer to him, his hands shielding his face while glaring at the boat whose spotlights were hot on them.

"Well, if it ain't the little guy himself," Anthony smirked.

"Screw you, Anthony!" the voice barked. The sound of a plank hitting the railing of their boat only emphasized his words. "I'm still twice the man ya are!"

"Yeah," Anthony laughed, "when I was three."

Although Charlie wanted nothing more than to choke Anthony himself for talking back, he was too busy wondering where Kate was. He peered cautiously at the cabin, and to his amazement, a dark figure slunk against the wall, untouched by the light that caught them.

"See," the voice continued, making its way across the plank. "If I didn't have orders, I'd skin ya alive and wear ya as a coat."

"I wouldn't be yer size, anyway," Anthony replied half-heartedly. "Too big and all."

The silhouette of the man came into view as he arrived on the fishing boat, the lights now behind him. He really was a shorter man, dressed all in gray with his hat cocked over one eye. "I swear, you've got a mouth on ya that'll get ripped off one day," he growled, his whole attention on Anthony.

Anthony scoffed, turning to Charlie and shrugging a little as he commented, "That's actually the nicest thing he's ever said to me."

"And the coat comment wasn't?" Charlie played along, trying to keep the attention on them while three more men boarded their boat, rifles in hand. His temple began to pulse as one of the men stood in between him and the cabin, the stranger's back unknowingly turned to Kate.

"Shut up, both of ya!" the man snapped. While his face was overshadowed by the bright spotlights, there was still an outline of crimson against his cheeks, evidence of his temper.

Anthony snickered but stayed quiet, and Charlie only stared at the man, trying to keep himself from peering at the cabin too much.

The stranger adjusted his jacket while adjusting his mood. "Now, I know ya got a broad stowed away on this vessel," he replied enthusiastically again, "who we'd very much like to meet."

The playfulness drained from Anthony's face. "Ya got what ya came for, Johnny. I suggest ya stay on track."

"Oh, I am," Johnny chuckled. "And it won't be hard to find her. We're on a damn fishing boat, for fuck's sake."

Charlie eyed the stranger next to him, figuring out how he could take him down while Anthony tensed up beside him. Johnny smugly stepped back, his eyes never wavering from Anthony. "Go check the lower deck," he instructed his comrades.

In that same moment, a female voice screamed, "GET DOWN!"

A hand caught Charlie by the collar of his neck, throwing him face first onto the floor. He slammed against the wooden deck with Anthony's grip still on him. The rapid fire blared from the cabin, stretching across the deck and striking the standing men with a shredding force. Charlie covered his head when he felt the spray of blood hit his face.

Something landed near him, and peeking up he found it was one of the armed men, the first to be mowed down by the gun fire. Stunned, Charlie looked at the cabin and detected a long barrel protruding out of the shadows, flicks of fire rolling out as the bullets continued to fly overhead. His chin scraped against the wood as he turned to check on who else had been hit, just as Kate's aim targeted the other boat.

One of the spotlights exploded into darkness as the gun fire hit it, immediately followed by the other spotlight going out in a blaze of sparks. Everything went dark, and all Charlie heard were screams and grunts as the men on the other boat tried to dodge her shots. Some fired back, but it was a wasted effort given how many pointless shots were fired compared to Kate's rampage.

Abruptly, the other boat's engine roared to life, and as it pulled away from the scene, its departure caused the *Sandy Patty* to sway. The plank that joined the boats skidded across the railing until it hit the side of the cabin, throwing it sideways. The wood cracked as it was broken and tossed in between the vessels, floating on the water as the trespassing ship crawled away with whatever remaining crew it still had.

The Tommy Gun eventually went silent, leaving someone groaning in front of him. While his eyes adjusted to the new darkness, Charlie realized that Johnny was hit but still alive, and Anthony's form was crawling to him. Charlie reached under his stomach, grabbed the handle of the revolver, and pulled it free. "Anthony, here," he called out, sliding the revolver towards him.

The revolver's silhouette caught Anthony's attention, and taking hold of it, he got to his feet when the Tommy Gun remained muted. With the sounds of the other boat's engine echoing in the distance, Anthony trudged freely over to Johnny. The other man was lying on his back, blood oozing out from his shoulder and abdomen. Anthony stood over him in the blurred moonlight, aiming the gun at his head. When Kate emerged from the cabin with the Tommy Gun firmly in hand, his confidence returned in full force.

Peering down at the dying man, Anthony couldn't help but smile. "Now, I know ya got a boss stowed away somewhere on these waters," he commented in the same mock enthusiasm Johnny displayed. "We'd very much like to know where he is."

"It don't matter," Johnny coughed, his body shuttering with pain. "He's got plans for you."

Anthony's jaw clenched, his finger on the trigger.

Johnny chuckled, a rumble of blood and laughter parting through his lips. "Little Anthony," he purposely stated, knowing that his rival hated to be called that. "Bet ya wished ya hadn't saved him."

Anthony gave the man his famous smirk. "From where I'm standin', I owe him a 'thank you.' Even found some booze to toast to him with."

"Go to hell," Johnny spat, blood bubbling out of his mouth as he spoke.

Anthony grinned a little wider, knowing that trying to keep him alive was no longer an option. "You first," he answered, pulling the trigger that caused a sharp *bang* to piece the air and Johnny's head to bounce off the wood as the bullet exited the back.

Anthony walked away from the body to help Charlie up who was too shaken by the incident to move. "Ya ok?" he asked as he pulled the younger man to his feet.

Charlie's blood-splattered face nodded as he looked around at the bodies littering the deck. "First gun fight," he awkwardly admitted, trying to keep himself steady despite the adrenaline rush that left his muscles rattling under his skin. His hat was on the ground next to him, and he gingerly picked it up. Surprisingly, he didn't remember feeling it get knocked off when Anthony threw him down to the ground.

"Ya did great, kid," Anthony congratulated him as he handed the revolver back before picking up his own hat off the ground, placing it back where it belonged. "Ya didn't die, so that's somethin'." He patted Charlie on the back, which almost sent him stumbling forward.

Anthony tried not to laugh at Charlie's nervousness, and instead ventured towards Kate, his own apprehension growing inside him. "Should I even ask if yer ok?" he questioned, pushing the brim of his hat up to see her better. He tried to keep the lightheartedness in his tone and actions so that it would mask the protectiveness he felt.

Despite the darkness and smoke, he knew she was smiling back when she replied, "I'm fine. My mother always said I was good with a typewriter."

Anthony allowed one chuckle to come out. "Oh, I bet she's real proud."

"Given the circumstances, she wouldn't be disappointed."

Anthony smiled, now understanding why she brought the bag on board. "So how did ya obtain that gun?"

The moonlight brightened as the smoke shifted from its path, and he was met with Kate's smirk, her face attractive underneath her scars. "You're not the only one who kept mob connections."

"Good girl," he remarked, winking at her as he walked over to the closest body and started dragging it to the railing.

"We're gonna throw them overboard?" Charlie asked, still standing in the same spot. He tried to wipe the blood from his face with his shirt sleeve, an act he never thought he would do given how much the shirt cost him.

"Best thing we can do," Anthony remarked, lifting the body over the railing. "Go ahead and get us outta here. Someone else could be close by."

With a nod, Charlie stumbled to retrieve the lantern Anthony dropped before making his way to the cabin. Hearing the body splash wrecked havoc on his nerves, and his hand shook as he hung the lantern back in place, the little flame still barely flickering inside. Getting behind the wheel, he tossed his hat to the side, catching a glimpse of Kate zipping up the duffel bag. She grabbed her cane as she stiffly stood back up, leaning against the wall to catch her breath.

Peering at him, Kate observed how white his face was. "Are you alright?"

"I will be," Charlie commented, turning the engine on which roared to life. He glanced back in time to witness Anthony pitching Johnny's body overboard. Shaking his head to stop the flood of panic, he slowly moved the throttle. The *Sandy Patty* glided back on course, quivering as if it, too, was still rattled by the attack. Charlie made sure to keep the pace slow so Anthony could toss the last body overboard without falling over himself.

But then suddenly Anthony yelled, "OH, SHIT! GUN IT!"

Charlie spun around as a spotlight came on in the distance. A horn blew as the size of the vessel became visible, revealing itself as a ship belonging to the Coast Guard. It was when he saw the second boat emerge that Charlie shoved the throttle forward, causing the boat to jerk and throw itself against the ocean waves.

Even over the engine, he could make out the high-pitched squeal of the skiff whose own powerful motor was helping it drive right towards them.

CHAPTER FOUR

. . . .

The minute Charlie slammed the throttle forward, the boat lurched out from underneath Anthony, causing him to fall backwards and tumble all the way to the stern. Air from the force of the speed caught hold of him, heaving his body over the side of the boat. He snatched the railing just in time, coiling his arms around the metal as his body slammed against the boat's side, his legs dragging against the water. His hat disappeared from the force, forever lost at sea. Looking over his shoulder, Anthony found the skiff keeping pace behind them.

Charlie, knowing he would lose Anthony if he went much faster, kept the boat at its quick and steady pace, risking that the skiff would catch up to them. Kate detected the hesitation, knowing it was because of Anthony. Without thinking about her bad leg, she dived for the duffel bag, ripping the zipper open and pulling a rifle and flat cartridge out.

With his eyes fixed on the dark path in front of him, it took a moment for Charlie to realize that Kate was holding the silhouette of a long rifle which seemed heavy by the way she handled it. He couldn't place exactly what kind of weapon it was, given the swinging lamplight and the speed of the boat he was directing.

"What the hell are ya using this time?" he yelled. They hit a wave, and he gripped the wheel tighter. He tried to keep things in line as the boat began to catch air in the front, lifting itself occasionally up off the water.

Kate kept her breathing even as she stayed focused on the task at hand, snapping a cartridge in place. "This is a B-A-R," she answered, remaining on the floor due to her leg.

"A what?" he questioned.

Kate huffed, "An M1918 Browning Automatic Rifle."

Staccato blasts cut the air, and Charlie looked back at Anthony who still gripped the railing. The skiff remained behind, their Tommy Gun lighting the space between them.

Anthony didn't know how much longer he'd be able to hang on. Suddenly, he heard the bullets hit the water right behind him, causing his anger to push back against his fear. "Sons of bitches!" he yelled over his shoulder at the skiff, trying again to hoist himself up over the railing. The boat's speed held him back, and the spray from the ocean made the rail slippery. He checked the cabin, seeing Kate with a rifle in her hand as she yelled something to Charlie.

The cold reality sunk its teeth into his chest as he realized she was going to act rather than stay out of the way. "Kate, don't do it! Stay right there!" he screamed.

Charlie could hear Anthony yelling, but Kate's voice was more coherent. The confidence she spoke with made him listen. "Where is the engine located on a boat like that?" she questioned, hoisting the strap of the rifle over her shoulder.

Charlie racked his brain for a minute, Anthony's muffled screams not helping. "Uh, it would be...in the back."

Kate stared out across the stern, past Anthony and at the skiff that stopped firing its weapon to reload. "Just keep this boat straight," she instructed Charlie. "I'm going to head to the front. When you see me wave my arm, you turn this boat to the right, and keep doing turns until you get that boat off our ass. Circles, figure eights, whatever. We need them in front of us."

"Got it," Charlie nodded, keeping his eyes forward while she crawled out of the cabin.

"Kate, listen to me for once!" Anthony demanded as he tried to loop his arm around the railing again after almost losing his grip. "Stay in that cabin or so help me—"

Kate ignored his threats as she crawled out of the cabin and to the edge of the boat, awkwardly pulling herself up on the rail. With the rifle still hanging over her shoulder, she used the railing to help her shuffle to the bow. The breaking waves were relentless as they sprayed up at her, making her unstable. Her auburn hair came undone from the jolting movements and thrashing wind, whipping around her face while she tried to keep a steady gait. Approaching the sandbags, Kate stationed herself as close to the front as possible.

Carefully sliding her jacket off, Kate transferred the rifle from one shoulder to the other as she worked. The cold air enveloped her as she wrapped her jacket around her waist and pressed herself as close to the railing as she could. She tied the sleeves in a double knot around the rail, securing herself to it. Moving the rifle back to her dominate hand, Kate pressed the butt of the gun tight against her shoulder. Taking a shaky deep breath, she looked at the cabin and began to wave her free arm.

Charlie slowed the throttle down when he saw her signal, steering the boat to the right and causing it to lurch sideways into a turn. Kate gripped the railing with her free hand, keeping the rifle pressed against her as she witnessed the waves come up the side of the boat.

Anthony used the tilted angle to his advantage. With all his strength, he lifted his leg up to the railing, trying to pull his whole body over. His abs burned and his cursing became more pronounced as he eventually lifted himself over, falling backwards against the deck. He barely had a chance to savor his victory when the boat abruptly veered left, throwing him into the railing again.

The engine roared underneath, deafening his ears as he staggered to his feet and shuffled clumsily towards the cabin, his adrenaline masking the aching in his muscles. "Where is she?" he called out to Charlie who stood white-knuckled at the wheel.

Charlie didn't have to answer him. Anthony caught sight of Kate through the glass, her lone figure tied to the railing. Beyond her, and coming towards them at a fast rate, was the skiff now facing them head on. Anthony fell to his knees before the duffel bag, pulling out the Tommy Gun and a fresh cartridge. Loading it, he staggered back to his feet and moved out of the cabin, finding that the skiff had already reached them.

Kate held her ground, taking the safety off as the skiff came into range. She fired quick shots at the front, each one producing four rapid succession of bullets as she pressed and released the trigger. The bullets sprayed the salt air and split the wood of the skiff's bow. In reply, the skiff began to fire pistol shots right back. Although a couple whizzed by, Kate firmly held the gun and laid her finger on the trigger again. The sound of cracking mixed with the rapid shots pierced the air as she aimed for the skiff's stern. Kate held on tightly to the rifle as it pounded against her shoulder, its fury pulsating as it continued on unwaveringly, tearing the stern apart.

The skiff was only halfway past them when the bullets penetrated right through the wood frame, slicing into its engine. The result was a burst of flame that shot out, blinding Anthony who was right in front when it blew up from the water. He covered his face and dropped to the deck as the explosion ripped half the skiff apart. The force pummeled the flat-bottomed boat forward, causing the front half to flip over and hit against the waves. The flames missed the *Sandy Patty* as the fishing boat remained on its own course. It had moved past the explosion at a speed that saved the boat from being scorched.

However, this didn't save it from flying debris, burning wood and ash spraying across the deck. Charlie dropped the throttle so that the fishing boat coasted along the waters. Bolting to the bigger flames, he smashed them out with his foot and threw the pieces he could touch over the railing. Luckily, most of the debris was smaller, the fires putting themselves out upon reaching the damp wood.

Still lying on the deck, Anthony lifted his head when Charlie finally reached him. "Ya ok?" Charlie asked as he helped Anthony to his feet, watching as the man rubbed his face.

"Yeah," he groaned, "just caught me off guard." Anthony blinked his eyes, his vision coming back to him despite the spots. He reached out and grabbed the Tommy Gun that was tossed out of his hands.

"Ya think they came from the patrol boat?" Charlie asked, eyeing the inferno that burned against the waves.

"Doesn't matter now," Anthony sighed, glancing over at Kate.

She still stood at the bow, her jacket tied around the railing, pinning her. The rifle slumped against her side, hanging from its sling while she held herself against the railing with one hand, the other clamped on the upper part of her arm, below where the butt of the rifle had been propped against her shoulder. He knew just by looking at the gun that it was going to leave a mark, her shoulder and arm bruised by its recoil. She might as well have been kicked by a mule.

"I'll check on her," Anthony announced, gripping the Tommy Gun securely and hoping to not lose it again. "Get us outta here."

Charlie perceived Kate's solemn appearance. He wanted to be the one to check on her this time, but being the only one who could steer the boat gave him a responsibility that he had to face again. Making his way back to the cabin, Charlie glanced at the burning skiff, floating in pieces. "What the hell did ya get us into?" he whispered, Lionel's image coming to mind as he went back into the cabin.

The engine groaned to life, and the *Sandy Patty* crept forward, slowly turning back to its main course. Feeling the vibrations rise from underneath the deck, Anthony approached Kate who had started to untie the sleeves of her jacket. He didn't bother to ask if she was alright this time. He could only watch with concern as she held her coat in one arm and slid the rifle off her shoulder, rechecking that the safety was on. Her movements were slow and careful, even deliberate, but her hands were shaking. He hated to admit it, but he loved the way her hair was tossed about her. He didn't, however, like the expression on her face, the way it had made her age so quickly.

Not wanting to make a scene, Kate simply handed the gun to him and commented, "This is becoming a longer night than I expected."

Anthony chuckled as he took the rifle and slung it over his own shoulder. She was touching her upper arm again, but dropped her hand when she realized he was eyeing her. "I knew it had a kickback, but I still wasn't ready for it," she tried to joke.

Anthony chuckled, but decided to leave the mood light between them. Gently touching her other arm with his free hand, he nodded to her, telling her to use him as a crutch, which she gave into without fighting. Quietly, the two walked carefully back to the cabin, falling into their own rhythm as they both caught sight of the skiff in the distance, the flames starting to burn out.

"We need to tell him," Anthony spoke up, stopping her before they reached Charlie. "Tell him who he's dealing with."

Kate's jaw clenched, a pain filtering up into her mind. "Why, because the last two encounters we had didn't say much?"

"I'm serious—"

Kate's shoulders dropped slightly which she forcefully picked up to throw her head back to look at him. "So am I. He needs to get that shipment back. Let's not complicate things more for him."

"It's complicated already," Anthony reminded her, taken aback by how she pulled her arm out of his grip and staggered away. "He knows we're out here, Kate. He's pulling the same shit you did—"

Kate stopped, and Anthony immediately swallowed the rest of his words. Slowly pivoting around, Kate's beautiful gaze lunged at him from where she stood. "And he still hasn't learned his lesson."

Anthony swallowed hard. "What lesson would that be?"

"Don't fuck with the woman who kept your secrets."

Anthony deflated as Kate turned away and limped into the cabin. Closing his eyes briefly, he took a couple deep breaths before he could follow her in, the rifle sagging against his shoulder.

Upon reaching the cabin, Charlie looked in Kate's direction to find her leaning against the wall, resting while she caught her breath. Her hair was damp against her face, and the pain was evident in the way her scowl set in. "Ya did it," he congratulated her, though his expression was anything but joyous.

Kate smiled a little, somehow still pretty even with the scars and the limp and the deadly aim. "High calibers are a woman's best friend," she remarked, quieting down when Anthony stepped inside to join them, staying mute while bending over to retrieve the bag. Charlie felt the strain in the air again as his attention fell between Anthony and Kate, watching as she gingerly put her coat back on to fight the chill in the air.

Witnessing how their moods were gradually deteriorating, Charlie began to blame Lionel, the responsibility now turning to disgrace. "I shouldn't have let ya go out there," he muttered, shaking his head. "I don't do that. I don't put people in danger."

"It's cute how you think you had a choice," Kate spoke up as she hugged the wall.

Charlie's jaw clenched, the silent rage building up, the same anger and torment his brother always brought out of him. "Enough people have died," he told her, looking directly into her eyes.

Although the conversation happened right next to him, Anthony stopped listening up to that point. He was putting the Tommy Gun and the rifle back in the bag when something wet slipped against his hands. As the dim lamp swung back and forth across him, it took him a moment and a long hard look to realize that blood was smeared across his palm and fingers. He knew it wasn't his, and that's when his heart pounded into his ears. He rose up, his eyes searching Kate until he noticed something dark dripping off the side of her hand. She hadn't put the jacket on because she was cold. She was hiding an injury.

Anthony stepped over to Kate, trying to match her nonchalant mood when putting the coat on. He looked at Charlie whose back was to him, his face forward again as he steered the fishing boat. Then his eyes fell on Kate, her weary gaze meeting his.

"I don't want there to be anyone else," Charlie was saying, keeping his attention on the water.

Kate continued to stare at Anthony who lifted his hand up to show her the blood. When her face twitched in repulsed guilt, Anthony's eyes hardened. "Tell him," he mouthed.

"I know he deserves what's comin' to him, but he's my brother. I can't just stand by and watch," Charlie continued on, ignorant of what went on behind him.

Kate shook her head stubbornly, pressing her lips shut.

Charlie scoffed at his own conversation. "But he had to keep things from me. He had to drag us all into this because he couldn't just tell me that our family needed help."

Anthony couldn't take it anymore. "This isn't yer brother's fault."

"Oh, yeah?" Charlie asked with skepticism, glancing over his shoulder. "Then whose fault is it?"

Anthony opened his mouth, but then he saw the betrayal in her eyes, and for a split-second he wondered if it was the same expression she had given *him*. Did she look this way when she realized who put the hit out on her over two years ago?

The words caught in his throat, and in the end all he could do was swallow them back down. "Circumstance," Anthony managed to say before he walked out of the cabin and stood at the railing. Defeated, he inhaled the salty air, wishing that some things had never happened.

Despite watching Anthony's reaction, the heat in Kate's face remained. She blinked her eyes so that her vision would stop blurring, tears threatening to expose her. She was glad Charlie remained facing forward.

"I think we're here," Charlie commented, pulling the throttle down.

With her arm and shoulder throbbing, Kate peeked out of the window to find the schooner growing in size as they approached, the truth burying itself in the back of her mind as their destination loomed in the distance.

CHAPTER FIVE

. . . .

The schooner stood out like a glittering pirate ship. Lights dotted from bowsprit to the top of the quarter deck like it had forgotten its freight and threw a party instead. It stood isolated against the black waters, a lonely paradise where the only law was the sea.

"Shouldn't they be actin' a little more inconspicuous?" Charlie questioned, steadying the *Sandy Patty* as they approached the larger ship.

"They're in international waters. They're free to advertise," Kate responded, trying not to focus on the pain.

Charlie grunted, but said nothing as he steered the boat past the schooner. Turning the wheel, they glided around to where the quarter deck was, seeing the painted name of *Shenandoah* imprinted below the dark windows.

The ship was still, and the lack of crew looking over the railings or appearing on its deck made the place a little eerie. Charlie pointed out to the rope ladder, tossed over the side towards the front. Kate attentively made her way to her cane that fell near the bag. Picking it up, she sucked all the air in to help muffle a cry that instead came hissing out from in between her lips. Limping out of the cabin, she came to a stop at the railing, panting while her strength started to falter. The boat underneath her began to veer to the side, Charlie directing the *Sandy Patty* closer to the ship. She stared up at the wooden sides of the schooner, waiting for someone to peer down at them which never came.

Realizing their boat was slowing to a stop, Anthony pulled himself out of his thoughts and looked around, taking in both Kate and the *Shenandoah* towering above her. He reluctantly walked forward, seeing how close enough she was to the rope ladder to touch it. Blood still dripped off her hand, which he watched her try to wipe off on her jacket, and so he undid his tie, pulling it from around his neck.

The engine shut off, the roaring suddenly eliminated. The *Sandy Patty* bobbed right next to the *Shenandoah* whose sails were down, the bare masts resembling a sharp pitchfork against the starry sky. Kate had the ladder in her grasp, though her other hand was becoming useless. She tried to ignore the pain by tugging on the ladder, checking for security. Satisfied, she was figuring out a way to ascend upwards when Anthony reached her.

"We need to do something about yer arm," he commented, holding up his tie.

"It's just a graze," Kate tried to tell him, but as he tenderly touched her arm to persuade her, she almost screamed. The pain left tears in her eyes, and she couldn't stop Anthony when he yanked the jacket off her shoulder. The tear in her blouse was now exposed, revealing the blood-soaked fabric. The bullet had gone through the side of her arm, possibly scratching the bone which Anthony figured must hurt

like hell. So as carefully as he could, he wrapped the tie around the wound to help stop the bleeding.

"Maybe ya won't die from blood loss now," Anthony joked before tying it off with a knot. He pulled her jacket back on, fixing the front so to hide her injury.

Kate hoarsely thanked him, and with careful movements, tried to reach for the ladder again. This time Anthony stopped her by grabbing it instead.

"No ya don't," he commented when she glared in bewilderment at him. "I'll go first. Ya can trail afterwards."

"I wish you'd stop babying me," she commented, anger boiling in her exasperated tone.

"Babyin' ya would be to tell ya to stay on this boat while we check it out, which I haven't done." Anthony kept his attention on the ladder as he climbed up on the railing. "Though, I should since ya got yerself shot."

Kate took an awkward step back to give him room, trying to mask the agony in her face by glaring up at him.

"I know this is gonna come as a shock," Anthony grumbled, waiting for her eyes to meet his before he continued, "but he's pissed me off, too. I know yer angry with him, but now is not the time to be lettin' it fester. We gotta get this shipment to land so this kid and his brother are off the hook."

"I'm not angry. I'm disappointed," she mumbled, which Anthony barely caught over the lapping of the waves against the boat's sides.

"Makes two of us," Anthony replied back. He wanted to say more, except Charlie's absence had become suspicious. Peering over at the cabin, he saw Charlie finally making his way from the lower deck. "Everythin' good?" Anthony called out, trying to mentally step aside from Kate's heavy conversation.

"Yeah, was checkin' the space," Charlie answered, approaching them with the rifle in one hand and a new cartridge in the other. "Think we should take some protection," he admitted, handing the gun and ammo to Anthony, who put his hand out for it so Kate wouldn't try to. He didn't want blood completely all over the guns just yet.

"Ya got that revolver still with ya?" Anthony asked, tossing the old cartridge out and placing the new one in before slinging the rifle over his shoulder.

Charlie nodded, and Anthony got down from the railing. "Why don't ya go up first, kid," Anthony suggested. "Be the lookout."

Charlie agreed by replacing Anthony on the railing. He pulled himself up on the ladder, and his body weight caused him to swing towards the ship. He collided lightly with its wooden side before starting his descent upwards. With heavy breaths, Charlie made his way up the schooner, and reaching the railing, hoisted himself over. Back on his feet, he searched the deck as he pulled the revolver out that had remained tucked in his waistband. Seeing no one, Charlie leaned over the railing and signaled for Anthony to come up.

"Ladies first," Anthony announced, the rope ladder now in hand.

Kate's hand shook when she moved it, doing her best again to wipe as much of the blood off as possible on the bottom of her coat. Anthony helped her to the railing, holding on to her waist as she moved upwards, positioning herself on the ladder. "I'll hold yer cane," he instructed as he took it from her, knowing she would have trouble climbing with it.

Grabbing the rope with her good hand, Kate put her foot on one of the rungs as she turned to face Anthony. "Why are you disappointed?" she asked, reverting back to their previous conversation.

"Honestly?" Anthony half-smiled. "Because I never had a chance with ya."

Even in the moonlight, he saw the amber-green of Kate's eyes. "Pretty ironic," she tried to smile, though turning away when the pain in her arm reminded her that her strength was dwindling. She took an agonizing step up the ladder when Anthony's voice came out softly behind her.

"And why's that?"

Kate didn't break from her attempts at climbing. "You always had a chance," she panted, wanting to see his face then. But looking down meant seeing how high she was and she'd never been a great fan of heights. So she deliberately focused on climbing up, her arm and shoulder pulsing in pain every time she tried to steady herself and grab hold of the next rung. Her leg almost buckled a couple times when trying to push herself up, and her head began to swim, making her nauseous. When she glanced up, she found Charlie peering over the railing, and she realized then that she was almost at the top.

"Now she tells me," Anthony mumbled, watching as Kate climbed. Seeing the way she struggled to keep hold of the ladder made him uneasy, but despite his feelings, there was lightheartedness in his actions. A sense of relief flooded his face when Kate reached Charlie, who helped her over the rail. With the ladder in one hand, Kate's cane in the other, and the rifle slung over his shoulder, Anthony began his ascent.

Charlie let Kate use him as a crutch when he helped walk her over to a pile of small crates that were stacked nearby. Kate, despite her anguish, gazed across her surroundings to find the entire front deck stocked with rows of crates. Beyond that, she observed the quarterdeck, the only part of the ship which didn't hold any lit lanterns.

Helping her sit down, Charlie grimaced at how pale she was and how the sweat was beading across her forehead. "Ya should have stayed behind," he commented, his meaning going as far back as to the beginning of that night.

"And miss all the fun?" Kate grinned, resting on the crates which neither helped nor hindered her physical state. "I'm somewhat responsible for why you're here."

"How are ya responsible?" the young man gawked, taken aback by her statement.

Kate closed her eyes, her head hurting so bad now that she didn't realize she had spoken out loud. "Because I was the bearer of bad news regarding your brother," she lied, looking up at him but only long enough to make him think she was being honest.

"This is my brother's fault, not yours," Charlie answered, his annoyance surfacing as he made his way back to the base of the ladder. "None of us should be here."

Kate bit her tongue while Charlie leaned over the railing to check on Anthony's progress. Her shoulder was burning as if the bruising was trying to compete with the gunshot wound. She looked at her hand and found blood still seeping down it, crawling almost to her fingertips. She was losing some sensation in her arm, and she had to grab her own hand to place it in her lap so the blood wouldn't stain the crates. The black fabric would absorb it, hiding the residue at least until the sun came up.

After helping Anthony over, Charlie gripped the handle of his revolver, apprehensive that no one had showed themselves yet. "I'm gonna go check the cabin. Someone has to be here."

Anthony nodded, pressing the rifle against his side as he made his way to Kate, handing her cane over. Watching Charlie leave for the cabin, Anthony surveyed the deck from where he stood.

"Ya still love Eddie, though?" he asked, his eyes wandering while his attention on her didn't.

His question forced Kate to pay attention to him, to stare at those blue eyes which made so many before and after her swoon. She heaved herself to her feet, pursing her lips to remind herself to keep her pain quiet. She straightened up as best as she could, trying to look Anthony right in the face. "I probably would," she admitted, "except hate is so much easier."

Anthony sucked in a sharp breath before exhaling it all out through his nostrils. "Don't let him win."

Kate might have responded if Charlie hadn't appeared then. To keep her mind off of the subject Anthony had sparked, she busied herself by slipping her useless hand into the jacket's pocket, hiding and protecting her damaged arm. She could feel something hit her fingers, and for a split second her mind registered that it was her small pistol, still buried deep in the pocket.

Anthony swallowed hard as he watched her, but didn't let his emotions show when Charlie stopped in front of them, his eyes wide with anxiety lining his brow.

"No one's in there," the young man announced. "Thought there was music playing from downstairs when I walked past the hatch, but I couldn't see anythin.'"

Anthony's adrenaline begin to skip. "They would have heard us comin', especially with that engine of yours."

"Go down below?" Charlie wondered, only because he wanted to be done with it all. He wanted to live through the night long enough to see his brother again so he could beat the shit out of him himself.

Anthony, curious about the crates since first seeing them, stepped over to one. After a couple attempts, he ripped one of the nailed boards off the top of it. Pushing some straw away, he found the top of a bottle which he pulled out of the crate and popped the cork. Taking a swig, he almost coughed when the liquor hit the back of his throat.

"The real deal," he spat as he wiped his mouth. He sat the bottle back in the crate before he addressed his companions. "That ain't been watered down. Someone's gonna make a lot of money off this."

"They wouldn't leave cargo like this unguarded," Kate stated, her vision growing fuzzy which she tried to blink away.

"Guess we better get this over with," Charlie commented, leading the way towards the hatch.

The hatch lay open before them, revealing a sturdy stairwell and light splashing against the floor. Anthony tried to peer in, and found no signs of movement. "This is the part I hate," he grumbled as he went down first, holding the rifle firmly in hand.

When his feet hit the lower deck, an overwhelming sense of déjà vu rushed over him. The lower deck was laid out with a handful of tables and chairs, illegal gambling set up to draw in new customers. In the chairs sat the crew and the prostitutes and what appeared to be a few customers, silent and unmoving. Anthony approached the nearest table, focusing on how well-dressed they were. Kate's cane echoed as she came down into the room, but his heart was already pounding in his chest by the time she gasped.

From face to face, he was met with their lifelessness; their glossy eyes and their silent deaths. They all died

differently: some shot in the head, some strangled, some punctured multiple times by bullets or knives. They were all placed there, playing games they wouldn't win, the victims of a floating speakeasy they couldn't escape from. Some bodies were unable to sit up anymore and had slumped against the tables. Anthony grabbed one of the men by the hair, lifting his head up enough to find that his throat was cut. The resemblance to Eddie's cousin came instantly to mind. Instead of letting the head fall on the table like he had once done, Anthony simply set it back down where he found it.

The music from the turntable in the corner played on in a jazzy stupor. Kate leaned against the base of the mast to keep herself upright. It was while surveying the faces she noticed one that looked too familiar, one with the same features as Charlie.

There was an odor in the room which foretold how long the bodies had been there, and Charlie was the only one who bothered to cover his nose. The shock of the mass grave made his feet feel heavy as he trudged forward-looking at the bodies. "What was goin' on here?" he asked, bewitched by the scene.

"Some ships throw parties like this to help draw in clients," Anthony's hoarse voice spoke up as he made his way back over to them. "We may have enough time to get outta here if we move now."

"What about the cargo?" Charlie questioned, dropping his hand from his nose. "My brother depends on this. We can't leave it—"

"Charlie," Kate spoke up, her full attention still on the body.

Neither of the men listened to her. "We may have to, kid," Anthony stated, interrupting him. "They've already been here, which means they aren't far away, just like last time."

"I'm not leavin' it!" Charlie snapped. "My brother's life is at stake, and I'm not about to waste this entire trip — "

"Charlie!" Kate said more forcefully, this time looking at him. Her eyes twinkled in the lamp light, and her face twisted into sympathy. Before either Charlie or Anthony could ask, Kate was shaking her head while turning back to focus on the table, on the face now ruining everything.

Both men followed Kate's stare. Cold anticipation slid under Charlie's skin as he moved forward, coming to a stop next to her and searching the faces. Slowly, he realized that one of the bodies had a very familiar profile.

Charlie's revolver lowered as he walked towards it, hypnotized as he rounded the table to view the person head on. He gazed at the familiar forest-green eyes, the slicked back dirty brown hair, the bronze skin still showing signs of bruising. The revolver dropped from his hand, landing on the floor as he stared at Lionel, the bruising around his neck revealing his cause of death.

"No," he whispered, his vision blurring as he made his way around to Lionel, his shock evaporating into panic as he began to cry, "No no no!" He grabbed Lionel's face, searching for any signs of breathing or pulse, but was only met with his brother's body slumping further back. Teetering, Charlie caught him before he slipped off the chair, and the brothers fell to the floor together. Charlie wrapped his arms around Lionel, cradling him as Lionel's eyes stared up into nothing.

Anthony and Kate both stood by helplessly as Charlie's tears streamed down his face, the sobbing beginning to rock out of his chest as he held on. "We weren't finished!" he screamed.

Anthony couldn't help survey the other bodies while Charlie's screaming overpowered the music that still played in the backdrop. "He's replicated it," Anthony mumbled, remembering when his friend was gunned down by the men on the roof, how the car exploded around the young blonde singer.

Kate cringed when he said the words. The disgust made her clench her jaw, and she turned away, shunned by them all. She had just passed Anthony and was heading for the stairs when Charlie's broken voice stopped her.

"Whose fault is it?"

Kate remained standing, leaning against her cane as the pain made her voice useless. She didn't turn around, though. She couldn't.

"Whose fault is it?" Charlie questioned again, seeing the cracks in her façade. "And what does that damn speakeasy have to do with all this?"

The floorboards under Anthony squeaked as he took a step back, putting Kate solely in the spotlight. She squeezed her eyes shut, trying to block them all out, trying to not give into the pain she had held on to for those long two years.

Charlie glared at her through his now bloodshot eyes. "Kate!" he snapped, demanding an answer.

Kate's own tears revealed themselves, the sobs shaking under her skin as her face twisted in pain. She gripped the cane as if it were the only thing that gave her courage, reminding her to stay strong for reasons no one else would understand.

"He has a right to know," Anthony spoke up, pushing her to respond.

With the jazz music humming in the background and the smell sticking to their clothes, Kate's whisper crawled out. "It's mine."

Charlie held his brother tighter, only able to stare out across the room at the woman who had known too much from the start.

"I told you what happened at that speakeasy was the beginning of this," her voice crooned while she rotated just enough to look at Charlie. "The Caprices didn't kill everyone."

"Who did they miss?" Charlie questioned, his eyes never leaving her.

"They didn't miss," Kate admitted, her voice rough as she tried to remain cold against his hot anger. "Someone survived."

Charlie's gaze shifted to Anthony, seeing if he would give anything away. But all he did was stare at the floor.

"Eddie," Kate's voice cracked into the room, "was the boss' nephew and my husband."

Despite the pain in his chest and the heavy weight in his arms, Charlie's mouth gasped open. The story regarding the nephew's wife came back to him, and that's when the scars on her face and the limp in her walk all started to make sense.

Kate's eyes shimmered only a moment against the light before she continued. "His family planned my death, used it as a tool to conspire against the Caprices, which Eddie carried out. He tried to gun me down while I was in a car. He thought I had died, but the problem was I didn't, and I took all his and his family's secrets to the Caprice family.

"But after seeing Eddie again, right before they attacked him in the speakeasy, I came to a realization," Kate's eyes darted to Anthony. "I didn't want to save him because I loved him. I wanted to save him because I didn't want to be like him."

Anthony, trying to keep his own emotions from surfacing, smiled a little when he nodded in understanding.

Charlie looked from Anthony to Kate. "So Eddie's the mob boss now? He's the one who did this?"

Kate gripped her cane, wincing as the throbbing in her arm and shoulder pulsed up into her temples. "None of this would have happened if Eddie had just died like he should have." She stared at Charlie then, her face starting to break. "And for that, I am so sorry."

Neither Anthony nor Charlie stopped her when Kate turned away and staggered back up the stairs to the top deck. Both men remained still, the creaking of the ship the only sound between them besides the jazz in the background.

"So you were there?" Charlie questioned, his grip around Lionel never lessening.

"Yeah," Anthony sighed. "Eddie and I were the ones who found the Durantes dead in the speakeasy, part of the little game the Caprices had made up. I had left him down there to face his fate when he admitted to Kate's death, even fired my gun to spook everyone to get 'em out of there. I was the reason the speakeasy was even exposed.

"When I reached the lobby, I snuck off to grab a Tommy Gun while everyone was in hysterics. I was told about a spot where they were usually stashed, and luckily they were still there. I figured once they were done with him, they'd try for me next and I wanted to be ready. I didn't want to spend my life runnin' from 'em, so I waited near the speakeasy's entrance. Instead, comin' out of the secret passage was Kate, back from the dead."

Charlie eyed him as he spoke, witnessing the glimmer in his eyes as if for a split-second Anthony was reliving those feelings when he had seen her.

"She asked me to go save him," Anthony continued. "And when she asked, I didn't hesitate. Eddie was my best friend, and part of me hated leavin' him behind. It would have been my biggest regret. Want to know why?"

Charlie shrugged, unable to ask.

"'Cause that's exactly what his family would have done," Anthony answered, his eyes burning with anger. "Despite his delusional fantasy of being accepted, they would have left him to rot for 'em. Don't get me wrong; I still hate him for it. But after seeing Kate alive, it made me think that maybe he'd get it through his thick skull that this whole mob lifestyle ain't what it's cracked up to be. So I went back down into the speakeasy and open fired on the men beatin' him to death."

Charlie stayed quiet, looking at Lionel and the strangled marks on his neck.

"He had died for a second," Anthony continued, "but I was able to revive him. I dragged him out of there, flagged down a taxi, and hauled him to the hospital. Paid off the driver so he wouldn't tell anybody, and kept things vague with the hospital staff so they wouldn't know who he was, or what really happened."

Lionel's body felt heavy in his arms, reminding him that some people couldn't be saved. Charlie peered up at Anthony, watching as he re-positioned the gun with his own regret hanging in the air.

"I don't work for the Durantes," Anthony admitted. "I'm just keepin' an eye on him. Keepin' enemies close, so to speak. But both Kate and I feel responsible for his demise, despite the fact he had asked for it." Anthony turned away then, giving up on making excuses and needing a break from the deadly finale around him.

Charlie had to ask one more thing: "What's he like now?"

Anthony didn't bother to look back. "He's a monster," he replied as he reached the stairs. "He's an ugly ass monster."

CHAPTER SIX

. . . .

The jazz continued on in an endless repeat that lulled Charlie into a callous state. Laying Lionel's body down, Charlie finally picked himself up off the ground, feeling a lost sense of reality overcome him as he came to his feet. His mind tried to find flaws and loopholes explaining why this wasn't Lionel; that he was still lying in a hospital bed, miles away from this body in front of him. Despite every angle and every attempt at making this body into a complete stranger, Charlie kept coming back to the hard question: how was he going to tell their mother?

The schooner creaked underneath Charlie's feet as the Atlantic rocked its waves against the ship's sides. The sounds scraped against his nerves, and he turned away, moving past the other bodies and dragging himself back up the stairs. His eyes took in each step as he lost himself in his thoughts, torn between finishing a job and killing everyone who had been a part of it. He had reached the last step when he looked up and realized two Tommy Guns were pointed at him, wiping his intentions clean.

Charlie staggered backwards from shock, though a hand stopped him, grabbing his arm and yanking him forward. He came to a jerking stop next to Anthony whose hands were folded behind his head, the rifle taken from him.

"Anyone else?" a voice asked, gruff yet easy to blend in among the armed shadows.

"Nope," Anthony replied, and for the first time Charlie sensed an air of failure about him.

Charlie did his best to distinguish between the intruders, but in the end he couldn't. His brain could only make sense that there were six of them, armed and all wearing black trench coats. There was nothing about them that stood out enough to be easily recognizable. He glanced at Anthony, who remained solemn and yielding, and then Kate, who stood on the other side of Anthony with one hand on her cane and the other still in her pocket.

"Hands up," one of the shadows demanded, to which Charlie begrudgingly mimicked Anthony. He closed his eyes, practicing Lionel's once popular technique by taking deep breaths and staring into his own darkness. But then voices broke into his haven, and he was forced to overhear one of the men harassing Kate.

"Ya tryin' to be defiant? I said raise yer hands."

Clearly the man was new to the scene, given how the rest hadn't bothered with her. Kate's voice came out smooth but forced, exhaustion dripping off her words. "And I already told your friends that I can't."

"The boss ain't gonna like ya goin' against orders."

"I'll take it up with your boss, then," she replied coarsely, never moving her voice above the monotone reply.

Charlie didn't bother opening his eyes, even when footsteps started running towards them. The guy was seemingly out of breath when he came to a stop. "She's gotta go back down and wait there. These two can help load."

He didn't see it, but the gruff voice who had been addressing Kate poked the end of his gun in her back, pushing her forward. Though she didn't make a sound, it was Anthony who knew she had caved under the harassment, her body hunched while she took a quick step forward to catch herself. While that one step showed her weakness, it also showed her stubbornness. Kate stomped the end of her cane firmly on the ground, straightened her back, and proceeded to take one aching step after the other.

Charlie tried to swallow the lump in his throat, hearing the cane's rhythm drawing closer to him. Anthony almost put his hands down to help before another Tommy Gun came up behind him, pushing its barrel up against the back of his neck.

Kate glanced at Anthony whose attention hadn't wavered from her despite the gun's interference. "Now you know," she told him, alluding back to their private conversation.

Anthony smirked, his smile charming against the surrounding hostility. "I always did. I just wanted ya to say it."

The barrel of the gun prodded into Kate's back again, pushing her forward when Anthony's words made her stop. For a split-second, she thought they were back in the days before mobsters, Eddie, and all those other girls. Back in those early days when their friendship should have taken a right turn instead of coming to a dead end.

Being led towards the stairs, Kate paused for a moment to catch her breath. Hearing her, Charlie peeled his eyes open enough to see her. While the lighting was dim in the cabin, her mint julep eyes held on to their sparkle. For a second, Charlie was staring at the mysterious woman in the mint green dress rather than the tormented beauty who now stood near him.

"It was nice meeting you, Mr. Rant," she tried to smile.

There was so much Charlie wanted to say to her, his bitterness tightening around his throat like a noose. He wanted to blame her, yet the scars she wore reminded him of her own escape from death. The longer he stared at her eyes, the more he saw the confidence that caught him off guard in the drugstore. "You as well, Katherine," Charlie murmured, keeping his answer simple so the chaos boiling underneath him wouldn't lash out at the wrong person.

Kate smiled a little at the intent behind the sensitivity, remembering those same feelings while lying in a hospital bed, frozen and heartbroken with her own hell fuming inside her. "Now you can see why they're a pain in my ass," she commented before being forced to turn away.

Charlie eyed her, turning a little when she began making her way down to the lower deck, her cane echoing along the stairwell. He closed his eyes so his thoughts wouldn't follow her, reminding him of who laid on the floor among the silent macabre and jazz.

Kate, however, was not allowed the same luxury. She kept her eyes down as she reached the base of the lower deck. Although she tried not to pay attention to the bodies trapped in their dead party, her peripheral vision was not so kind. Their forms stood out in the lamp light, mannequins in a scene set just for her. Two men followed her into the room, and they pushed her towards the base of one of the masts without any concern for what surrounded them.

Without warning, one of the men yanked her hand out of her pocket and pushed her up against the pole. She gasped and cried as they forced both her arms to wrap around it. She felt both her shoulder and arm burn in protest while sharp metal suddenly dug into her wrists, informing her that she was being handcuffed.

Kate squeezed her eyes shut, burying her face into the wood when the tears began to show. It was while she was in her dark, painful world that the footsteps creaked down the stairwell. They were off beat compared to the jazz music still swirling lazily in the air, unfazed by the grave situation. The grunting came before the monotone beat of a different cane, and her skin prickled when he drew closer, the tapping reminding her of what they had done to each other.

He limped forward, his broken legs fused in place so he could move, his arms healed but stiff, his once gallant gait now jagged and often hard to maneuver. There was, however, a certainty about him that she detected when he stopped in front of her, the hero still somewhere inside the villain.

His voice was gentle despite the sarcasm threatening its edges. "Welcome to hell, baby."

Kate's eyes flickered open, moist and torn as she saw his face, barely recognizing him except for his gray eyes and the way he parted his blonde hair. The reconstruction made him look average, but hardened. However, he was there staring at her with that remorse look she had last seen him with, down in a speakeasy before he was taken by the Caprices. Tears rolled down her cheeks in response. "Eddie," she whispered.

Eddie rotated to the side and glared at the men. Taking the hint, the men walked back to the stairwell to wait. Turning back to face her, he lowered his tone more. "I'm gonna be honest with ya. This isn't what I wanna do."

That tone. It sounded just like how he used to be.

Eddie, his mouth drooped on one side, pronounced his words distinctly to hide the struggle in speaking. "I deserve what I got, everythin' down to the death ya had Anthony save me from. I know ya told him to do it. He couldn't take all the credit.

"But like I said, I'm gonna be honest with ya. These boys have seen your face. They understand what ya mean to me. If I let ya walk outta here, they might one day use ya against me. I'm not gonna have that hangin' over me. If I let ya walk, then I showed them I have empathy and can be softened. I can't have that either. So please believe me, sweetheart, my actions are purely business. This is nothin' personal."

"It was personal to me," she whispered. Despite her attempts at hating him, she stared at the version of Eddie who stood in the speakeasy, the one who was handsome and hopeful and intact. But then she remembered Charlie, and his brother who lay a few feet away. It reminded her of her old self, a young wife who was gunned down in a car by her husband who tried to kill her because his family had told him to. "It was personal to a lot of people," she added, her voice finally faltering as it fell into weakness from all the memories.

His hand touched Kate's cheek like it used to, except his fingers weren't all straight from the way the bones had healed. "This isn't about revenge," he cooed to her. "This is about survival."

Kate moved her cheek out of his hand, resting her forehead against the wooden mast. She couldn't deny she was in love with his memory, but the man who stood before her wasn't him anymore.

"Ya have to understand that the death my enemies would give ya would be horrific. They can't know you're alive. So this is the best I can do, given the circumstances."

"Put a bullet in my head," she murmured coldly. She was tired of hearing him talk.

Eddie's face shifted, repelled by her words. "Believe me, Kate. You'll thank me for this."

Kate blinked up at him, keeping her mouth shut despite wanting to scream like she had when she realized the car was going to run itself off the dock and into the river.

"No matter what," Eddie added before turning to leave. "I have always loved ya. Just believe that. Maybe after this life we'll be allowed to love each other the way we were meant to."

Kate didn't respond, too hardened by life choices to yield to empathy. By the way he nodded at her silence, she knew he understood. There was now a mutual understanding between them, where words held no value. While watching him hobble away, she stared after a man she could neither live with nor live without.

The sudden blasts from a rifle deafened the room, and Kate's eyes automatically closed as her ears begin to ring. In the darkness, the familiar firepower of the B-A-R blasted holes in the floorboards and splintered the wood. The loud shots moved about the room, shivering up her spine and making her stomach turn. The water sprayed out of the ship's wounds as the man cleared the rifle's chamber, and Kate only opened her eyes when the footsteps finally moved past her. She witnessed the last man leaving a lone lantern on a table near her, the jazz music still playing as the water began to cover the floor.

The pain in her arm and shoulder were causing her muscles to spasm, and Kate's forehead pulsed with sweat as the trembling set in against the handcuffs. She eyed her surroundings, the bodies still sitting around her with their spirits waiting just on the other side. The panic began to rise up her throat as she was forced to face the death she thought she escaped from. It was when the water started creeping up against her feet that she buried her face into the wooden mast and screamed. She screamed like when the car started sinking into the Hudson river with the two dead bodies in the front seat.

Her scream trailed up after Eddie, bursting out of the hatch and into the night air. Anthony and Charlie caught it over the sounds of the gangsters ordering them to help grab the crates and stack them on the *Sandy Patty*. Charlie begrudgingly continued on with his work. Anthony, however, listened to the gunshots being fired, and watching one of the men walk across the deck with the rifle in hand had turned his alarm into rage. He caught sight of Eddie staggering to the railing of the schooner before being helped down by his goons. The sight of him made Anthony viciously aware of what had happened below deck.

"I think they blew holes in the ship," Anthony muttered under his breath. He stepped down into the *Sandy Patty's* lower deck and stacked a crate right next to Charlie. "They're gonna try drownin' her again."

Charlie pretended not to hear him. He didn't want to think about his brother, or Kate, or even the crate he just sat down. How would he tell their family, that Lionel had been murdered, that his body was in a ship headed for the ocean floor? It made him sick and exhausted at the same time, and all he wanted to do was run far away and forget that any of this ever happened.

"Kid, snap out of it," Anthony hissed as they both went back up the ladder, passing the gangster who stood lounging at the wheel. They both moved towards the railing as two more crates were lowered with rope, one on top of the other. "We've all lost someone—"

"He was my brother!" Charlie barked, confronting Anthony head on which caused two of the gangsters to turn their attention to them.

"Ya got a problem?" one asked, his finger already hovering over the trigger of his gun.

Charlie's round eyes blazed red, and he didn't blink as he backed away from Anthony. "Not yet," he grumbled, flattening his tone as he moved back to grab the crates that were being lowered.

Anthony eyed the gangsters, who motioned with their heads to get back to work. Straightening himself up, he stepped forward to help Charlie. As he untied the rope, he mumbled, "Why did yer brother do all this in the first place?"

Charlie didn't want to answer him, despite the words already tumbling out. "Our Pa's losin' the family business."

"Then I guess all this isn't a waste after all."

Charlie glared at him, taking the comment personally. Anthony undid the rope, and Charlie snatched the top crate before Anthony objected. He moved by the gangster who eyed him, and rushed down the ladder's steps as best as he could, eventually slamming the crate down on top of another one. He seethed through his teeth, closing his eyes so the spots would leave his vision. Anthony came up beside him, hearing his crate being set on the floor next to his stack.

"Kate was right about one thing," Anthony whispered. "If ya don't finish this, all this death will be in vain, especially yer brother's."

Charlie sniffed back the emotion that tried to seep back into his eyes.

"Yer family still needs ya. Yer brother started this for them. Ya need to finish it."

Charlie peered at Anthony, trying to be standoffish despite the lecture hitting him. "So what are *you* gonna do?"

"Me?" Anthony smirked, his old playfulness returning. "I'm gonna go get my girl back."

"Need any help?"

Anthony shrugged his shoulders. "Ya scratch my back, I'll scratch yers."

Charlie nodded, the closest thing to a handshake he could think of.

Both of the men trudged back up to the main deck, and to their disappointment they found Eddie stepping off the ladder. "Ya know, Anthony," Eddie proclaimed, rotating around to face his old friend. "Even after two years, your confession still rubs me raw."

Anthony placed his hands on his hips, breathing heavily from the exertion. Eddie staggered forward to approach him, and Anthony's hard expression didn't look much different from when he left Eddie by himself at the speakeasy, gun in hand and telling him to face his demons alone.

"I guess some things haven't changed," Eddie continued, noting the expression as well. He came to a stop in front of Anthony, though keeping a slight distance.

Anthony knew it wasn't just his expression he was referring to. It was Kate, the bodies, the one night of hell...

"Guess not," Anthony reluctantly answered, not bothering to hide his disgust. Knowing the fishing boat was almost full and watching the men climbing down the ladder made him anxious. He glanced at Charlie, who was keeping a stone-cold demeanor as he too watched with apprehension. The schooner was starting to appear lower, filling with water all while Eddie wasted time with psychobabble. "Guess ye'll be crawlin' back down that hole ya love bein' in," Anthony commented, wanting to get rid of him.

"It's all I've known," Eddie responded, his throat raspy from the cold air.

"Sure," Anthony scoffed. "Like I always told ya, Eddie. Ya need to live a little."

Although it didn't look like it used to, Eddie smiled. He casually put his hand in his pocket. "You've told me a lot of things, a lot of truth that was sometimes hard to hear."

Anthony eyed him, part of him knowing he was solely addressing Kate now. "Should I have censored myself?"

Eddie chuckled a little. "No. In fact, you've said so much while I said so little. I never really thanked ya for savin' my life." Eddie pulled his hand out of his pocket and stuck it out for Anthony to shake.

"Kate saved yer life, despite what ya did to her," Anthony snapped back, unable to contain himself.

"Believe me," Eddie answered, and something in his eyes flickered. "I'm thankin' her as well."

Anthony stared at his oldest friend, anger and disbelief causing him to lose any quick response he might have had. He still couldn't get over the way Eddie looked now. It was the other reason he felt so uneasy around him, why he didn't stick around long enough to know these minions that surrounded him or taking a stance in the hierarchy of his misfit organization. Eddie's face had been rearranged by the baseball bats that were used on him down in the speakeasy. It reminded Anthony of when Eddie had the same technique done to a beautiful singer's beau. Lillian, with her cute looks and country-born accent, would always be an unknown starlet who went up in flames. And by flames, he meant the car bomb that went off when she tried to start the ignition.

But now, at that moment, Anthony needed him to leave. So he shook Eddie's hand instead of wasting any more time. It only took him a brief second to realize that, in between Eddie's fingers, was something small and metal; something that felt like a key to a pair of handcuffs.

The realization shined on Anthony's face, but before he gave himself away, Eddie responded with, "Wait until I leave. Then she's all yours."

CHAPTER SEVEN

. . . .

"We got too many crates, boss. Both boats are full."

Eddie watched the man who approached him, the last one who stepped off the schooner. "That's fine; we've got plenty. We'll take this little fishin' boat back first. Stay here with the other boat to make sure this schooner has been submerged, along with these two gentlemen," Eddie instructed, nodding to Anthony and Charlie as he spoke.

The gangsters succumbed to the demand, half of them remaining while the others climbed back up the ladder. The boat that originally brought them there was stationed on the other side of the schooner, turning the ship into a bridge between the two smaller vessels.

With his men following instructions, Eddie addressed Anthony for the last time. "I'm sure a fast boat like this can outrun the Coast Guard."

Anthony stayed silent while a knot formed in Charlie's stomach, both of them heeding the warning. For Charlie, though, the act was more personal. Not only had they taken his brother, but now they were going to take his boat.

"Hope ya don't mind," Eddie addressed him, looking into Charlie's face with some compassion. "This is a remarkable boat."

Charlie's voice came out in a deep and threatening tone. "Ya better enjoy it while it lasts."

Eddie smiled a little, glad the kid still had some fight left in him. "Oh, I will," he replied. "Now, if ya don't mind, I've got places to be."

Charlie scoffed at the comment, turning his back on the mob boss as he made his way to the ladder. Anthony followed, the handcuff key burning in his hand.

"I'll take good care of it, Charlie," Eddie called out with an odd kindness that usually didn't follow a man in his position.

Charlie, however, took it as a fake sincerity. "Fuck off," he mumbled, grabbing the ladder and climbing angrily up.

"I like him," Eddie decided, looking at Anthony who stared back with his own perplexed gaze. "He reminds me of me, especially when I was once in the same position."

Anthony smirked a little, stepping over to the ladder to follow Charlie.

"You'll always be my best friend, Anthony."

Anthony stopped. He remembered those words, the same ones he said in the speakeasy when his eyes gazed on the pistol he carried in his hand. *You will always be my best friend, Eddie. Despite my feelings, I'd still go to hell and back for ya. You were the only family I had.* A sad smile lifted the corners of his lips, realizing he really meant what he had said.

Looking over his shoulder at Eddie, Anthony nodded and left it at that.

Charlie climbed over the railing when Anthony started up. He had made it halfway when the loud engine of the *Sandy*

Patty started up, and the fishing boat rumbled away from the schooner. Anthony quickened his pace, and the minute he climbed over the railing, his instincts heightened when he found the deck to be deserted.

"We gotta get Kate," Anthony whispered, making his way to the hatch. He reached the opening, and turned around to make sure Charlie was behind him. But he wasn't; he remained by the railing, his own fear expressed in the lines of his worn face.

"I can't go down there again," he answered, the pain of seeing his brother floating in the water petrifying him.

"Then find somethin' we can use as weapons," Anthony instructed before jogging down the steps and into the water-filled room.

The holes that were created brought in a strong amount of water, and by the time Anthony reached the end of the stairs, he was waist-deep in its freezing clutches. He shuddered as he waded forward, holding his own tension back as a couple of the bodies floated to the surface. He caught sight of Kate, handcuffed to the mast with her head buried against the wood. He worked against the water which tried to paralyze his limbs, and didn't think twice as he moved a beaded gown whose occupant was lying face down in the black surface.

"Kate," he called out, realizing she hadn't looked up. He quickened his pace, and finally upon reaching the mast, he found her shaking uncontrollably.

"Just hang in there," he told her, finding her wrists and desperately shoving the key into the lock. Twisting it, the handcuffs popped open, and he took them off, noticing even in the dim light how much the metal cut into her skin.

The silence in the room was colder than the water. While Anthony moved around the mast, he came to a sudden stop, finding Kate looking up at him from behind an ashen face. Kate's head lightly fell against the wood, though her eyes never left him. She breathed heavily but didn't say anything.

"You gotta stay with me," Anthony encouraged as he held her around the waist and pulled her from the mast. He forced her to put her good arm around his neck for stability, in which a hoarse cry escaped her lips.

"I'm sorry, but I ain't leavin' ya here," he answered back, awkwardly dragging her through the water.

Kate almost couldn't feel her arm, which terrified her even more. Everything was cold and pain, and for a moment she couldn't distinguish where one began and the other ended.

"Don't give up, ya hear me?" Anthony questioned. "Don't roll over now and play dead for him."

"Anthony," Kate tried to say, though it came out weak and airy.

"Don't 'Anthony' me. I know that tone," he responded, coming to a stop and forcing her to look at him. "I'm tired of goin' to yer funeral," he admitted sternly, "so yer just gonna have to make it outta here, whether ya like it or not—"

"Could you stop?" Kate tried to say, but her voice was overpowered by his.

"Ya don't fight this hard and then give up cause ya saw his face," Anthony continued on. "There's more to life than him and this feud you two have."

Kate only had one option left. She took her good hand, and with all the strength she had, slapped him across the face.

The surprise attack caused Anthony to stumble to the side, his momentum hard against the water that lapped around him.

"Don't," Kate spoke through shivering lips, "don't ever take my silence as weakness."

Cradling his cheek with his hand, Anthony's stunned expression gave way to his infectious smile. "Noted," he replied.

Kate huffed out a deep breath that was an imitation of an irritated sigh, but then her leg gave out and she sank into the water before Anthony grabbed her, pulling her back up.

Flinging her arm back around his neck, Anthony pushed harder against the seeping ocean with Kate's weight against him. Upon reaching the stairs, Kate forced herself up the steps, and Anthony made sure she had her footing before he followed behind. He was just pulling himself out of the water when a sizzling sound snapped behind them. The lamp was now extinguished from the rising water, submerging the rest of the room into darkness. And in the background the jazz music continued on until the melody was slowly drowned, finally coming to an end.

Climbing out, Anthony dragged Kate over to where Charlie was, on his knees in front of some liquor bottles. "What the hell ya doin'?" Anthony asked, sitting Kate down on a remaining crate next to where he was working. The smaller boats really hadn't been able to fit them all; there was still at least a third of the shipment remaining.

"You'll see," Charlie responded.

Anthony peered into the opened crates Charlie had broken into, finding that the ship not only hid rum but French Champagne, whiskey, and English gin. Then he saw the jars of clear liquid, and his eyebrows shot up. "Moonshine?" he gawked.

"Right ya are," Charlie answered, a gleam of mischievousness lighting his tired face.

Anthony's eyes searched him over, watching as Charlie held the mouth of two champagne bottles together. One was cleaned out and intact while the other bottle was positioned on top, half broken. He was using it as a funnel to pour a jar of moonshine through, using his hand to make sure the majority of it stayed in the bottom bottle. While watching him work, Anthony caught sight of the champagne bottle next to him that was already full.

"I'll need somethin' for a fuse, though," Charlie commented, satisfied by how much was in the bottle and tossed the broken bottle off to the side. "Like a cloth or somethin'."

Charlie eyed Anthony and Kate, who stared back at him sopping wet from their excursion below. "I'll take care of it," he mumbled, ripping off the sleeves of his shirt.

"Need help?" Anthony offered, to which Charlie gave one of the ripped sleeves to Anthony, along with one of the filled champagne bottles.

"Twist it and stuff one end in the bottle until it reaches the moonshine. Leave the other end out like a fuse. We'll soak some of it in the leftovers so we can get a decent flame goin'."

Anthony twisted the cloth enough so it would go down the neck of the bottle. "You've got a real knack for this, kid," he commented as he worked.

"My ma would have my head for this, but I'll take the compliment."

Anthony laughed, which was broken by Kate's shaking voice. "I don't mean to rush things, but we've got company."

Both men looked at her and then out over the railing, finding a patrol boat gliding towards them. The sound of a boat engine started up on the other side, and both realized too late that the remaining boat had also heard the Coast Guard.

"Good thing I made two," Charlie commented. He dipped the end of the cloth in the left over moonshine before

trading it with Anthony's, who was wiping the moonshine residue off the bottle with his shirt.

With the dried off bottle in hand, Anthony brought out his lighter from his inside pant pocket, and after several attempts, was able to attract a flame. "I'll distract the boat. You take care of the patrol," he instructed, lighting the end of the cloth before tossing the lighter at Charlie.

The moonshine caused the cloth to ignite, and running to the other end of the schooner, Anthony skidded to a stop at the railing. He found the fishing boat Eddie had given up starting to pull away, the name *Beatrix* painted on its side. Putting all his momentum in his throw, Anthony slung the flaming glass bottle at the *Beatrix*'s deck. On impact the glass shattered, and the burning moonshine splattered across the deck in flames. Yells erupted, and the engine was shut off. Anthony watched as two men tried to extinguish the flames with their feet and jackets. Another disappeared into the cabin while the driver remained behind the wheel, not knowing what to do since the fire was hovering on the boards over the engine.

Anthony pushed his sleeves up, but before he jumped overboard, his name was being called from behind. Pivoting around, he found Kate dragging herself after him. She was hunched over now from where she stood, tossing something at him which he fumbled to catch. Looking down, he found her small pistol, the same one she pointed at him earlier.

"They never did search me," she smiled, resting against the crates for support. "I've always loved this coat for its deep pockets."

Anthony held the pistol in hand as he asked, "Does this mean I still gotta chance with ya?"

Kate, despite the exhaustion pulling her in, kept her smile as she replied, "Don't die and you will."

With a wink, Anthony turned and climbed over the railing. Taking a couple quick breaths, he dove into the water.

Watching as he started his swim to the boat, Kate stumbled back to Charlie who was trying to start the lighter again. She noticed that the schooner was starting to tilt a little, the water below making it off balance. What she didn't notice until it was too late was that the patrol boat was running their spotlight across the deck, finally landing on her.

Charlie looked up just as the light hit her, and became more concerned when she didn't duck out of the way. She just stood there, staring into the blinding light like a moth to a flame. "Kate! Get down!" he called out.

"Put yer hands in the air!" someone from the patrol boat yelled.

Kate remained how she was. "Is it almost lit?" she asked calmly, her voice foretelling the somberness that was setting in.

Charlie smiled a little, understanding that she was creating a diversion. In response, he flicked the lighter in rapid succession, holding the moonshine-soaked cloth over it.

"Put yer hands up! We will shoot you!"

"Charlie," Kate pressed, her voice easing into fatigue.

Charlie cursed under his breath just as the flame sprang up, lighting the cloth into a bright torch. Dropping the lighter, Charlie darted towards the railing, throwing back his arm that held the glass bottle. When his feet came to a halt, he propelled the fire and liquor into the air. In almost a perfect arch, the lit bottle sailed into the night sky until it smashed right on the bow. Burning moonshine swelled across the wooden deck, covering the front of the ship like lava as the flames leapt up from the alcohol it was consuming.

Kate stood there staring, her gaze only diverted when Charlie grabbed her and forcefully pulled her away, draping her arm around his neck to help her move faster. Gunshots punctured the air after them as he half-dragged her to the other side of the deck, each step she took becoming more and more listless.

Looking over the railing, they both found that the *Beatrix* had moved a distance away with a small fire still burning on the deck. Two of the men were still trying to put it out while Anthony wrestled another man at the bow. The driver was rounding the cabin when Anthony punched his opponent in the face and dived for something on the deck. When he lifted himself partly up, Anthony shot aimlessly at the driver with the pistol he regained, grazing the man and causing him to slide back into the cabin. Anthony tried to shoot the guy who was wrestling him, but the man was a brute force that kicked him in the arm, knocking the pistol back out of his grip.

Charlie checked the side of the ship, disturbed at how much water they were taking in. They didn't need to jump too far to reach the sea, which he was quietly thankful for, given how exhausted and wounded Kate was.

"I won't be able to swim," Kate reasoned, leaning against the railing as the hopelessness became reality.

"I'll jump first so I can catch ya," he told her.

She swallowed hard as she stared at the dark waters below them.

"Kate," the young man insisted, making her look at him. "We gotta pick our battles, and this is one we'll be pickin' together."

Kate acknowledged with a light nod of her head, feeling too subdued to answer otherwise. With time pressing on them, Charlie jumped from the railing, landing into the cold waves which embraced him. He shot out of the water, almost yelling from how cold it was. Wiping his face, he looked up to find

Kate gingerly crawling over the railing before she lost her grip and fell backwards into the sea. Charlie dived under the water when he didn't see her surface, and he was blinded momentarily, reaching out in the darkness and catching hold of her coat. He pulled her towards him, and with his body he helped push her up. They both broke through the surface, gasping for air while the *Shenandoah* sank behind them, rolling slightly on its side as it was dragged under the ocean waves.

Charlie, who was afraid the sinking ship would suck them down with it, looped his arm around Kate's chest and pressed her back to him. He began to swim sideways towards the *Beatrix* when one of the masts crashed to the left of them, sending waves rolling underneath and dragging them away from where they needed to be. Frantically, and with his own limbs burning, Charlie put everything he had into swimming towards the fishing boat. Although Kate was losing exhausted, she tried to use her good leg to kick, trying to help.

Meanwhile, Anthony was having just as bad of a time. Weaponless, he resorted to using his body, throwing punches that the opponent couldn't always block. He was able to knock out the first guy after a couple hits. But then the driver came out of hiding again, hitting him right in the kidneys which made him almost cave to his knees. Anthony only remained on his feet because Kate and Charlie had crossed his mind. The sinking schooner was now a reminder that he needed the boat to get Kate to a hospital and Charlie to his payoff with the Caprices. Gaining some strength back, he threw a punch, knocking the guy unconscious and over the railing.

Stumbling to the fallen pistol, Anthony picked it up again and made his way to the stern, finding two men still trying to extinguish the rest of the fire. One of the men came at him, which he shot on the spot. The other one, however, lunged

at him which made him aware that he was out of bullets. The
two tackled each other, slamming into the cabin as they fought.

Noticing the fight happening at the stern, Charlie swam
to the bow to avoid the confrontation long enough to help get
Kate on the boat. "Kate," he called, finding her eyes were
closed. They fluttered open, looking at Charlie with a glassy
stare.

"I'm gonna climb up, then I can pull ya over. So you're
going to need to keep yourself afloat until I can get up there,"
Charlie explained. "I know it's hard, but you're gonna have to
try."

Kate nodded despite her body screaming it couldn't.

Charlie let her go, trying not to watch as she bobbed in
the water, doing what she could to keep herself afloat.
Knowing he was losing time, Charlie tried to reach up for the
railing, but he was too low in the water to reach it. With no
momentum, he kept trying to toss himself upward, each time
failing to even come close. Running out of breath, he was about
to try again when Anthony leaned over the railing, nose
bleeding and one of his eyes already swelling in the corner.

"Need a hand?" he asked wearily, holding his hand out.

Charlie, without responding, grabbed Kate and made
her go first. Anthony clutched her arm while Charlie tried to
push her body up, helping Anthony obtain the momentum he
needed to pull her over. Once on deck, he laid Kate down, and
then went back to the railing to help Charlie. He had helped the
young man just enough for him to grab the railing when the
guy he had knocked out came back to life. Attacking from
behind, the man wrapped his arm around Anthony's neck,
dragging him backwards against his will.

With all his strength, Charlie scrambled over the railing.
He was about to run at the guy who caught Anthony when

Anthony instead rammed his elbow into the side of the man's stomach. He crushed the top of the man's foot with his heel, and threw his head back into the man's nose, blinding him and causing him to stumble backwards.

"Get this boat movin'!" Anthony spit out, and Charlie realized why. The spotlight of the patrol boat was moving past the last of the *Shenandoah*.

Running to the cabin, Charlie started the engine and began to pull away when the patrol boat demanded for him to stand down, the fire he started now out cold. Without hesitating, Charlie pushed the throttle, springing the boat to life in a roar as the propellers launched the boat forward.

Kate, swimming in and out of consciousness, rolled onto her stomach and peered out across the deck to where Anthony was beating on the last man. Trying to push herself up with her one arm, she collapsed back on the deck as if she had never tried. The need to reach him made her persistent, and she dragged herself forward using one arm while her wounded arm remained limp. Her vision blurred as Anthony knocked the guy out again, this time hurling him overboard. She had stretched out her hand in wanting him when everything went black and her body collapsed.

Anthony lurched back, faltering from his own exhaustion despite being proud he had taken on the men and had been victorious. Grinning, he turned around and found Kate stretched out across the deck, her hand still reaching for him. His smile disappeared when he realized she wasn't moving, and cold panic threw him towards her. He fell on his knees by her side, moving her to her back and finding her lips had stopped trembling.

"Kate!" he screamed, trying to feel for a pulse that his panic couldn't find.

Helpless, he picked her up in his arms, holding her against him as the windswept over them from the speed of the boat. His eyes burned with tears as he looked out, watching the world moving out of control. The waves bumped along the sides, the sea mist hitting him in the face, and all Anthony could do was hold on to the girl he could never have.

Charlie was too caught up in outrunning the Coast Guard to notice anything but the man going overboard. He saw Anthony holding onto Kate at the bow, but Anthony's cries were muffled against the beating of his own adrenaline which steered them back to land. When the spotlight finally became a dim light in the background, he laughed in triumph, proud of himself. He continued to drive on, keeping the boat's speed up as best as he could. Knowing Kate's condition made any attempts at slowing down and checking on her pointless. They had to reach land, no matter the cost.

He remembered the two gangsters in the hospital then, and tried to recall the port they had named where the shipment needed to be dropped off. He didn't know the port, so they had told him landmarks to follow: head West, and upon seeing two white buoys, make a slight right and watch for the headlamps. Charlie was nervous that he had over guided the boat when racing from the patrol boat. So when the two buoys came into sight, he breathed a sigh of relief and headed in the direction he had been told. Land soon appeared, little dots of light separating the city from the rural.

Charlie finally slowed the engine down in order to regain his bearings, and he moved the boat towards the docks that were approaching in the distance. There were no signs of any headlamps being on, but maybe he had misheard that detail, he wasn't sure now. Realizing that neither Anthony nor

Kate had moved, he turned the engine off and went to the bow to check on them.

Anthony cradled Kate in his arms, his eyes outlined in red as they brimmed with tears. Charlie drew closer, taking in the scene and watching the expression on Anthony's face as it stood out in the moonlight, knowing all too well how he felt. "We're almost there," Charlie told him, his voice quiet against the sound of the sea.

"They'll kill me," Anthony murmured, staring out into nothing. For a second, he was in the darkness of the speakeasy. The cold waves of remembrance hit him like the rapid fire of the Tommy Gun that had been in his hands, firing at the baseball bat-slinging mobsters with Eddie lying in the middle of them. His blood had been everywhere, his life a mere flicker left in his shallow breaths. Anthony glanced down and instead found Kate, just as lifeless as her husband had been.

Charlie bent down, feeling for a pulse which he found. "She needs a hospital," he confirmed, and turning to observe their destination again, he saw the docks were now illuminated by automobile lights that were leaving a trail of spotlights against the shore. "I can take her," Charlie told him. "Now's yer last chance to run before they realize who ya are. It'll be a hell of a swim, but it's not impossible."

"No," Anthony decided. "I lost her once. I'm not doin' it again. I wanna be here for it."

Anyone else would have thought he lost his mind, but out of respect Charlie nodded and went back to the cabin. He turned the engine back on and directed the boat forward, pulling into the docks as the silhouettes of men in suits came into view around them. Anthony picked up Kate, standing tall with his face still slightly bleeding and his eye almost halfway closed. He remained silent as he held her, hearing the engine shut off and watching Charlie drop the anchor and throw ropes to two well-dressed men who tied it to the dock.

"Looks like you had a rough night," a man called out from land. When Charlie looked over the railing, he found a fine-fitted suit lighting a cigar.

Anthony continued to stand in silence, and Charlie stepped forward to put the plank in place. "Here's your cargo. We could only fit what we could," Charlie told the man with the cigar as he made his way down to the dock, hoping to take some of the curious attention away from Anthony.

"Who's that guy?" the man asked, not easily distracted as his gaze fell on Anthony, watching as he walked the plank with Kate still clutched in his arms. He squinted a little before he added, "And what happened to Kate?"

Charlie kept his eyes forward, watching the man puff on his cigar. "He's a friend who came to help. We ran into some trouble, which Kate got caught in the middle of."

"Poor thing," the man commented, though still eyeing Anthony. "He knows her?"

"Yeah," Charlie said flatly. "It's why he's here."

The man shrugged a little as he pulled out a thick envelope from the inside pocket of his jacket. "Well, a friend of Kate's a friend of ours."

Charlie tried to remain calm as the man passed him the envelope before turning to tell two men near him, "Take these three to the hospital now. And wrap her up in somethin' warm."

An overwhelming sense of relief flooded through him, even despite the numbing loss still hibernating in his chest. "Did ya see 'em take my brother?"

The man sighed, and there was a sense of defeat in his actions as the cigar smoke blew out in the air. "Yeah, kid. They slit two of our guys' throats when they snuck in and got him. By the time we learned what happened, they were long gone."

"I found him," Charlie answered, his eyes blazing with anger as he moved past the man. "They terminated his services for ya."

Although the man remained unfazed, he didn't hide the mumble under his breath. "Yea, we figured they would."

While the mobsters were already peering into the lower deck, confirming that the cargo was there, Anthony approached the dock. Shifting Kate a little in his arms, he proceeded to follow Charlie, passing by the mobsters who came to transport the liquor. All eyes fell on him, though none lingered long enough to recognize him as the man who helped their enemy escape two years ago. He silently thanked the black eye and bleeding nose for disguising his face.

Charlie reached the car first, holding the door open as Anthony slid into the back seat with Kate still resting in his arms. Closing the door, Charlie marched around the back and got in from the other side. He placed Kate's legs on his lap so he could sit in the back seat next to Anthony. Two mobsters got into the front seat, the driver quickly starting the engine and steering the vehicle away from the docks. The front seat passenger handed Charlie a blanket.

Charlie draped the blanket around Kate, though Anthony still refused to release her from his hold. Working around him, Charlie tried rubbing her legs to see if any warmth would reach her while Anthony only sat there, preparing himself for the worst. He wished he had said something a little more romantic to her in that lower deck instead of running his mouth about things that just didn't matter anymore. He was staring at her pale face when her eyelashes fluttered, attempting to stay awake despite the cold pushing her back and forth into unconsciousness.

"Damn, they did a number on her," the man in the front seat commented, staring at Kate before moving his sights to Anthony. "Did a number on ya, too. Anyone left we can get our hands on?"

Anthony hesitated, wondering if Kate actually heard the man by how her eyelashes kept fluttering, trying to stay conscious. At that point it was fear or anger keeping her alive.

And Anthony knew exactly who would have caused both.

"One," he mumbled. "There's always one."

ACKNOWLEDGMENTS

. . . .

To my loved ones and supporters:

This story couldn't have happened if it wasn't for each and every one of you, for your overwhelming support and encouragement, and for your love of stories that made me always want to impress you with mine. I'm extremely grateful for you all, and will never be able to express my gratitude enough.

Regarding this novella, I have to give a special thank you to the following people who have helped it along the way: my mother, my Aunt Susan, and my fellow writers Gina Engman, Sharon Gibbs, Jim Kennedy, and Sarah Zama. Also, a very special thank you to Dean Samed who again astonished me with another brilliant cover. Thank you!

A. M. Dunnewin grew up with a taste for mysteries and thrillers, inherited ever so lovingly from her family. With a B.A. in Psychology, she's a gambler of words, obsessed with chai tea, and addicted to books—everything from classical literature to graphic novels. Her other hobbies include art, history, music, and watching classic films. She currently dwells in Northern California.

For more information, visit amdunnewin.com, or find her across social media on Facebook, Twitter, Instagram, or Pinterest.